I0590933

Liberating
Mrs. McBryde

Captive Western Widows

Cheryl Wright

Copyright

Liberating Mrs. McBryde

(Captive Western Widows)

Copyright ©2024 CHERYL WRIGHT

Small Town Romance Publications

Editing: Sarah Lamb Editing

ALL RIGHTS RESERVED

Without limiting the rights under copyright reserved above, no part of this publication may be reproduced, stored in or introduced into a retrieval system, or transmitted, in any form, or by any means (electronic, mechanical, photocopying, recording, or otherwise) without the prior written permission of the copyright owner of this book.

This is a work of fiction. Characters, places, and incidents are a figment of the author's imagination. Any resemblance to actual events, locales, organizations or people living or dead, is totally coincidental.

- *This book was written by a human and not Artificial Intelligence (A.I.).*

- *This book can not be used to train Artificial Intelligence (A.I.).*

Dedication

To Margaret Tanner, my very dear friend and fellow author, for her enduring encouragement and friendship.

To Alan, my husband of over forty-nine years, who has been a relentless supporter of my writing and dreams for many years.

To You, my wonderful readers, who encourage me to continue writing these stories. It is such a joy knowing so many of you enjoy reading my stories as much as I love writing them for you.

Table of Contents

Chapter One

Wild Ridge, Montana, 1880

Whit Starkey stormed into the saloon, gun in hand. "Where is she, Jensen?" he demanded, shoving his gun far closer to the saloon owner's face than he knew the man would be comfortable with.

"R…room five," he stammered as he cowered in the corner. Jensen reached for the key, but Whit didn't have time for that. His best friend's widow could be on death's door.

"I swear," Whit snarled, "if so much as a hair on her head has been harmed…" He didn't have time for this. Not now. Not when Bonnie McBryde was locked up in a room against her will. Jensen had gone too far this time. If women were willing to become prostitutes, that was their business. When Jensen took it upon himself to kidnap and drug them for his own evil purpose, that was another thing altogether.

Whit cursed under his breath as he hurried to the room where Bonnie was being held. Not that it could be much worse, but she was still wearing her widow's clothes. Still mourning. And Jensen thought it was fine to drag her to his house of ill repute?

His heart hammered in his chest. Angus McBryde would be enraged. Whit promised Angus as he lay dying to look after his wife. Only eighteen months later, and this happens.

Whit swallowed down the emotion that threatened to overtake him. He prayed Bonnie was untouched by the evil men who frequented this house of horrors.

Pistol still in his hand, Whit kicked the door. It barely shifted. Cursing under his breath again, Whit was more determined than ever to get inside. He kicked it again and again until finally the door gave way.

The smell of stale vomit hit him. Whit knew that meant not only had Bonnie been brought here against her will, but she'd been here several days. That was Jensen's MO. He would drug the women repeatedly for days on end until they complied. Locked in a room with no light and nowhere to go, they eventually gave in.

If they didn't, he didn't care. He would send a client up to teach them a lesson. One they never forgot.

Whit shuddered. Had Jensen done that to Bonnie? His heart thudded as he glanced down at her laying on the bed. She was naked apart from her undergarments. His heart thumped. Who knew what she'd been through. Or what they'd done to her.

He gazed at her and silently prayed.

"Bonnie," he whispered, shaking her gently. She didn't move. He touched a hand to her cheek. It was warm so she was still alive, which was a relief. "Bonnie," he said a little louder, but she still didn't respond.

Whit had no choice—he wrapped a sheet around her, then lifted Bonnie and threw her over his shoulder. He would get her out of this evil place if it was the last thing he ever did.

"What's the verdict, Doc?" Whit asked the moment the town doctor entered the waiting room. Whit was annoyed the man refused his request to stay by Bonnie's side.

"She's been drugged, as we suspected," he said, wiping a hand across his chin. "Probably laudanum, but I can't be sure. She will have to sleep it off."

"That's all?" Whit asked, not wanting to mention the obvious. Angus would never forgive him, and Whit was certain his friend was glaring down at him right now. He would be cursing Whit even more than Whit had already done himself.

Doctor Robert Tantor studied him with sad eyes, then reached out and put a hand to Whit's shoulder. "As best I can tell, she hasn't been harmed."

Whit almost collapsed with relief. There was no doubt in his mind—he had to take Bonnie home with him. He had to protect her as though her very existence depended on it. He was convinced her life was at stake, and he would not allow anything to happen to her. "Can I see her?" he asked, his voice full of emotion.

"She's still asleep," Doc said, "but I suppose it would be alright."

Whit stepped quietly into the room. Bonnie lay on the examination table, a blanket over her. His heart felt hollow at the thought of what could have happened.

He knew exactly what he needed to do, but Angus would not be happy. Whit knew he wouldn't. He wasn't even certain Bonnie would go along with the plan. She had always been strait-laced and followed the rules.

Whit was the opposite. *Rules? Who's rules?* That was his philosophy. He didn't care one iota for regulations or other people telling him what to do. As for propriety, it really irked him.

It was why he mostly kept to himself. Angus had always been like Whit—it was one of the reasons they were best friends. As he glanced down at Bonnie, he recalled the day the two men met. Well, they were boys then. Angus's family had immigrated from Scotland. It took forever for him to understand Angus with his strong brogue, and he teased the heck out of his new friend about it.

Thankfully, Angus understood he did it out of love, and wasn't being mean. They'd been friends ever since. There were a few years in between where Whit became a bounty hunter. Not by choice, but he was desperate for money and knew how to handle a gun. Angus was a wrangler, and a good one.

When he'd had enough as a bounty hunter, Whit came back home, and the two men purchased a ranch together.

Quiet moaning pulled Whit out of his musings. He reached out and held Bonnie's hand. It was soft and oh so small. He lifted it to his face in a caress. Loving Bonnie from afar had been difficult. His best friend had kept her away from him, worried Whit would claim her first. It almost threatened to destroy their friendship.

He'd known Bonnie from a young age—they'd attended school together. Well before Angus had landed on the shores of America. And yet, he'd claimed Bonnie for himself as soon as they were both old enough.

It was like an arrow to the heart for Whit. Not that he'd told Angus. Their friendship was worth far more to him.

Bonnie's eyes fluttered open. She snatched her hand out of his grip, then opened her mouth and screamed.

~*~

Whit sat with his head bowed as Robert Tantor explained.

"I can only guess at what's happening, but I'd say she recalled when she was kidnapped. I've given her a low dose of laudanum, and that should help. Is there anywhere you can take Mrs. McBryde where she will be safe? Somewhere she already knows and won't be unsettling for her?"

There was only one place Whit could think of, but wasn't certain Bonnie would agree. Especially since she had always been one for propriety. He glanced up at the doctor. "I can take her back to my place."

Doc Tantor stared at him. "Will she agree? Could it be a problem?"

Whit knew the doc was right. He also knew it was the only place he could keep her safe. "Then I'll have to convince her. I wouldn't put it past Gus Jensen to try and kidnap her again. Bonnie is a beautiful woman." His voice trailed off on his last words. She was the most beautiful creature he'd ever set eyes on. It pained him to see her in those dull black clothes she'd worn since Angus was gunned down by rustlers. Whit had managed to maim both, but they'd never been caught.

That didn't bring back his friend. His last words still shook Whit to his core. "Look after my Bonnie, no matter what it takes."

Whit knew what Angus was telling him, and he'd avoided it all this time. Now he had no choice—it had to be done. The moment she was well enough, he would broach the subject, but already knew how she would react.

It wouldn't be good.

Chapter Two

Bonnie abruptly sat up.

Where was she? The last thing she recalled was being dragged to the saloon by that vile Gus Jensen. After that, nothing. Her mind was foggy, which could be a good thing. Or not.

She glanced about. The room looked familiar, but she couldn't place it. The door flung open, and a man stepped inside. Relief flooded her. Doc Tantor. She recalled hearing his calming voice amidst the fog. He'd reassured her she was safe, and away from harm.

"Ah, Mrs. McBryde," he said as he stepped slowly toward her. "How are you feeling?"

In the shadows behind the open door, the silhouette of a man was visible, and she flinched. Doc Tantor closed the door and hurried to her side. "You're safe here," he told her in that quiet voice she'd gotten used to while still in a drug induced stupor. She glanced toward the door. "That's Whit Starkey. He rescued you, and has been here ever since."

"Rescued?" She was still confused about why she was here. The sheet slipped down to her waist and a cold breeze hit her. Bonnie gasped as she looked down. "Why am I…" She felt the blood drain from her face. Tears filled her eyes then ran down her cheeks. "What did they do to me?" she whispered, feeling unsteady. She laid back down again, and the doctor came to her side. He held her wrist. At first, Bonnie believed he was steadying her. It took only moments to realize he was checking her pulse. She glanced up at him expectantly. "What's the verdict, Doc?" she asked, her voice barely above a whisper.

"Not surprisingly, your pulse is a little fast." He let go of her wrist and stared down into her face. "As to the other question, I believe you were spared any improprieties." He patted her hand, and Bonnie felt immediate relief. There was a gentle knock at the door, and the doc turned to Bonnie. "Do you feel up to seeing Whit Starkey? He's been here for several days."

"Days?" She couldn't be more shocked at his words. "How…" Her heart thudded. "How long have I been out?" Her voice got softer by the word.

"It's only an estimate, but I'm guessing more than a week." He stared at her in that fatherly manner he always radiated.

"A week? Oh my goodness." She was more than exasperated, Bonnie was shocked. How could she lose a week or more of her life and not know it? There was another soft tap at the door. The doc stared at her. "Let him in," she said, then ensured she was completely covered before Whit was allowed to enter.

The lines on his face and the stubble on his chin told Bonnie more than words ever could. "Whit," she said on a sigh. "I don't know how to thank you." Tears ran down her cheeks the moment his arms went around her. He held her so tight she could barely breathe.

"I'm sorry, Bonnie. This is all my fault."

She pulled out of his arms. "Did you kidnap me? Or coerce Gus Jensen into doing so?" She pierced him with her gaze. There was no malice on her part. Bonnie knew who the culprit was, and it certainly wasn't Whit.

"You know I didn't. Angus would kill the man if he were still alive. I was sorely tempted," Whit said, then mumbled a few words she couldn't decipher. Bonnie was certain they were curse words. Dear Angus always used that method to cover up his swearing. They were like two peas in a pod, and it had torn Whit up when Angus was killed. He studied her. "I've collected some gowns from the boarding house. You'll be coming back to the ranch." Whit looked guilty for a man who had nothing to feel guilty about.

She stared into his face and pursed her lips. "What aren't you telling me?" she asked firmly. Although she had an inkling what it might be.

Whit rolled his shoulders, then took a step backwards. "I've made arrangements with the preacher," he began, but she interrupted him.

"No, no, no," she said under her breath. "Angus would not approve!" The sheet slipped down, and Bonnie grabbed at it, her heart pounding.

Whit held the sheet up around her, ensuring her modesty. "You're wrong. Angus would definitely approve. His dying words were for me to look after you." He swallowed hard. His next words were full of emotion. "The only way I can do that is to marry you."

After a long hot bath at the doc's, Bonnie felt like a new woman. Her head was still a little fuzzy, but it was getting better by the minute. After the initial shock, she knew Whit was right. Bonnie chose her favorite gown to get married in.

When Jensen abducted her, Bonnie's life flashed before her eyes. It was clear why he wanted her, and what he'd intended to do with her. She never wanted to feel like that again.

Whit had freshened up, and looked better than he did earlier. He was clean shaven, his hair had been cut, and he wore fresh clothes. "I collected all your belongings from the boarding house," he told her firmly. "I should never have allowed you to live in town alone." Regret was all over his face, but it had been her decision, not his.

"It was my choice, not yours. Until recently, I've been fine. Nothing untoward happened. Not even once." It was true. She'd worked at the mercantile, and at the end of the day went home. No one had approached her. Not even once.

Until Gus Jensen.

Even in her drab widow's gown, the man had attacked her. Did he think no one would miss her? As it turned out, it was true. No one noticed her missing for three days, according to the doc. Thankfully Whit asked after her at the mercantile, and discovered she hadn't turned up for work. He told Bonnie he'd known exactly where she would be.

She glanced down at her colorful gown. It was pink with a row of lace sitting right above the hem, along with a lace panel on the bodice. It was the first time in eighteen months she'd worn anything that wasn't black. It felt good.

"You look beautiful." Whit reached for her hand. "Are you ready?"

Bonnie nodded. "As much as I'll ever be."

They stepped out of the doctor's office and onto the street. With every step, her heart pounded. Bonnie convinced herself she wasn't being disloyal to

Angus. His final words told her Angus wanted her protected. Until today, she didn't believe it was necessary and had told Whit as much every time he checked up on her.

She glanced across the road toward the church. Her eyes strayed toward the saloon that sat further down the road, and a shudder went through her.

Whit stepped into her line of view. "Forget all that," he said, lifting her chin with his fingers. "Today we start over. Just you and me."

Bonnie knew she couldn't forget—not her short-lived married life with Angus nor her ordeal with the saloon. She knew, however, Whit was right. Today had to be the beginning of something new.

He held her hand tightly and led her across the road. As he knocked on the door to the vicarage, Bonnie felt her nerves creeping in. The last time she'd stood at the door of the preacher's home, it was with Angus. They were blissfully in love. She had no such feelings for Whit Starkey, but knew what they were about to do had to happen. Otherwise, how could he protect her from the likes of Gus Jensen?

That was Whit's argument, and she couldn't deny it. She'd tried it her way, and failed miserably. To his credit, Whit didn't remind her he'd tried to talk her out of it. The three lived happily on the ranch together after she and Angus had married. Bonnie still owned half, but refused to live there with Whit.

Propriety was important to her. He'd wanted to marry her back then, but Angus's death was too raw. Even now, it cut her to the core.

"Ready?" he asked as the preacher led them through the house and into the church.

"There are a number of ladies in the church cleaning," Preacher Johnson said as they entered. "Are you happy to have them as witnesses?"

"Absolutely," Whit said firmly, not giving her a chance to respond.

It wasn't long before they were husband and wife and on their way home. Bonnie wiped at a stray tear. *I'm sorry, Angus*, she said silently. *You are the only man I'll ever love.*

Chapter Three

Bonnie trembled throughout the entire ceremony. Whit knew it was not because she was cold. She'd been through so much, and he felt like a heel forcing a marriage on her so quickly. They both knew it was the only way he could keep her safe.

He couldn't risk Gus Jensen kidnapping her again. Second time around he could be successful. The thought sent a shiver down his spine.

If Whit hadn't gone to the mercantile for his monthly supplies, and asked about Bonnie, he may never have known she was missing.

Why her employer didn't report the fact, he'll never know.

He shook himself mentally and helped Bonnie onto the wagon. Every touch, every brush of her hand, sent shock waves through him. Whit was ashamed. Angus wanted him to look after his wife, but not like this. He didn't want Whit to marry her.

This marriage would be difficult. Not only for him, but for Bonnie as well. Whit knew Angus and Bonnie were deeply in love. It was obvious in the way they looked at each other, the way Angus held her when he thought they were alone, in every little thing they did.

Bonnie would never feel that way about him, and would never forget her dead husband. His memory would be forever engraved in her mind. Whit knew it would be difficult. For both of them, but especially his wife.

His wife.

Would he ever get used to thinking about her as his wife? Probably not, but he had the license to prove it was true.

"What about my room at the boarding house?" Bonnie asked out of the blue.

"All sorted. I packed up all your belongings and paid what was owing. Mrs. Crenshaw wished you all the best." It wasn't quite that way. The woman was more than a little upset to be losing a paying customer. She wasn't even convinced they were to marry. Whit had paid for an additional month to calm her suspicions. "I told Frank you wouldn't be back."

"You quit my job without asking me?" Her voice was so high-pitched Whit flinched.

"Bonnie," he said quietly as he settled himself next to her. "It is not safe for you to stay in town. Living out on the ranch at Rocky Point, well, we both know it's too far for you to travel into town each day." He frowned then. "Not that I want my wife working."

"I guess," she whispered.

This was not the Bonnie he knew. She had always been a strong woman, not one to give in easily. Still, Jensen knew what he was doing. The method had worked for him before.

Whit swallowed down his emotion. If he let it, his feelings would overtake him. Where would Bonnie be right now if he hadn't found her in time? He didn't even want to think about it.

"Are you alright, Whit?" she asked quietly. "You're pale." She reached across and placed a hand on his arm. It sent shock waves through him, but Whit knew he couldn't give in to these feelings. He promised Angus to look after Bonnie, not to fall in love with her. Little did Angus know it was already too late for that. He'd fallen for her when they were teenagers, long before Angus came on the scene.

"Just thinking about..." He paused. How could he say the words out loud? Bonnie was no doubt upset and worried about the situation she'd found herself in. Through no fault of her own. "I'm fine," he told her instead. "There's a blanket under the seat if you're cold." He reached down and pulled it out, handing it to her. Bonnie's fingers brushed his wrist as she reached for it, then spread it out, covering both of them. She scooted closer to give them both good coverage.

This wasn't his intent. Whit planned to keep his distance. Have no physical contact. That way he wouldn't dishonor Angus's memory with Bonnie. More than anything, he had to ensure she never forgot him.

"I suppose nothing has changed on the ranch," she said.

It wasn't a question, and Whit wasn't sure if she expected an answer. He answered anyway. "Not a lot. It needs a woman's touch for sure." He glanced at her then. When she and Angus lived there, the place was always spotless. The aroma of food permeated the living areas, and it was a joy to come home after a long day of work.

Since she'd left, nothing was the same. The ranch house was an empty shell of what it had been before. He rarely cooked for himself, and if it wasn't for the cowpokes, he probably wouldn't have eaten. They ensured he never went hungry. He had a dozen or so hens clucking around the place, so eggs were aplenty.

Still, there were decent supplies on the back of the wagon, and the root cellar and pantry both had supplies from before Bonnie left. What condition they were in was another question altogether.

They drifted into an uncomfortable silence, but it was better than trying to find something to talk about. Many a time they'd driven this route, but always with the three of them. Never only two.

He glanced across at his bride to see her eyes glistening with unshed tears. Whit wanted to reach across and pull her close against himself. He even let go of the reins with one hand, holding it tightly with the other.

Then he thought the better of it. *No physical contact.* That's what he promised himself. For Bonnie's sake, he needed to stick to the plan. She wouldn't want that either. In her marriage vows to Angus, she'd said the words that meant everything to her—*til death do we part.* She wasn't to know that would be a mere eighteen months later. For Bonnie, Angus was still alive in her heart. Whit was certain of it.

They reached the archway to the property, and Whit pulled up at Bonnie's sigh. "Are you ready?" he asked without thinking. Of course she wasn't ready. Last time she'd been on the property her husband had been murdered. She closed her eyes momentarily, then shivered. Bonnie leaned into him as though she needed comfort.

Whit had no choice. His arm went up around her, and a tear rolled down her cheek. He brushed it away.

They sat there for what seemed a lifetime. Bonnie was not ready for this. Neither was he. Both their lives were about to change, but Whit would stay true to his beliefs—that no matter what, he could not take Angus's place in Bonnie's life. They would live as a married couple, but never would they consummate their marriage.

The very thought of it shattered his heart. No matter how much he denied it, Whit was in love with his wife. Had been from the moment he set eyes on her. Only Angus had been the one to claim her. Despite all that, they'd remained the best of friends.

To the bitter end.

"I'm sorry," Bonnie whispered, her eyes wide. "I… shouldn't have done that." She straightened, and brushed at her cheeks.

Whit missed her warmth against him when she moved away. No longer was she close to him on the wooden seat. Now she ensured there was a gap between them. As much as he didn't want any physical contact, he craved to feel her next to him. He stared down into her face. It was twisted in pain, and mirrored the way he was feeling. "It's not a problem," he said abruptly, then lifted the reins. They began to move again.

In the distance Whit could see the ranch house. In the past, it had been a place of comfort. Now he dreaded arriving home. Things were tense between them already. What would it be like once they were inside? He didn't even want to think about it.

The ride down the long driveway seemed to take far longer than it ever had before. Except for the day of Angus's funeral. They'd ridden together that day too, and not a word was shared between them. Bonnie was covered head to toe in black, and until today, she'd continued to wear those dull and unflattering outfits. Propriety demanded it.

Now they were married, and she was able to put them aside and wear beautiful gowns again. He'd taken all her widow gowns and donated them to the church. She wouldn't need them for a very long time. Hopefully decades. Whit wanted to have a lifetime with Bonnie. Have children with her.

He glanced across at her and wondered what Bonnie was thinking. Did she want children? She had not produced babies for Angus, so perhaps she was barren? Or was Angus the problem? Whit had no idea about any of this—he'd never asked his friend. His private life was exactly that—private.

His heart thudded. None of that would ever happen. His vow of no physical contact would see to that. So why was his mind pushing all these possibilities toward him?

Because deep down Whit had always wanted a brood of children. A family of his own. He knew now that would never happen.

He pulled the wagon to a stop in front of the ranch house. As he climbed down, Buck, his foreman, ran toward him, relief on the man's face.

"Praise the Lord," he said breathlessly. "I had decided to come looking for you tomorrow." His hand went to his heart, and Whit was convinced the foreman's heart was racing.

"I apologize," he said, putting a hand to Buck's back. "Circumstances caused the delay." He leaned in and whispered so only Buck could hear. "I'll tell you about it later."

"Mrs. McBryde," Buck said, genuine pleasure in his voice.

Bonnie glanced from Buck to Whit, then her face crumpled. Buck turned to Whit. "What's going on?" he asked quietly, and was pulled aside by his employer.

"We're married. Bonnie is now Mrs. Starkey."

A low whistle left Buck's lips. "I'll let the others know," he told his boss who was also his friend. "It's obviously a sore point."

"Hopefully not for long." He strode to the other side of the wagon to help Bonnie down, but she was already in the process of climbing down. "Careful!" he said, then reached out and grabbed her, pulling Bonnie into his arms as she slipped. She stared up into his face, tears still lingering on her cheeks.

It broke his heart to see her upset like this, but there was no way around it. When Jensen made a decision, he was persistent. Whit was not a killer, but he'd defend Bonnie to the death if it came to that.

He slowly put Bonnie to her feet, then wiped away her tears. He reached into his pocket and handed her a handkerchief. It wasn't pretty and frilly like women liked to use, but it was practical, like its owner.

"Thank you," she whimpered. Whit felt her pain. Bonnie's pain was his pain. It was as though they were one person. Wasn't that what married life was all about?

Not this marriage. It was a charade. This fake marriage might be the worst thing he'd ever done.

Chapter Four

She'd been to this place many times before. Heck, she'd lived here for all of her married life. Today, though, it made her teary. Bonnie's memories of life with Angus came flooding back, and it overwhelmed her.

When Whit held her in his arms, time seemed to slip away. For a moment, she imagined it was Angus holding her, but reality quickly set in. She and Whit had been friends before Angus came on the scene, and Bonnie had always believed he was the one. She saw a marriage in their future. Except it didn't happen.

She'd loved the two men equally, but Whit had slipped into the background. He was the more loyal of the two and refused to compete for her attention.

With her heart pounding in her head as well as her chest, Bonnie glanced up the steps toward the front door. This would be a huge turning point in her life. Most of all, she wouldn't sleep in the room she'd shared with Angus. She would move into Whit's bedroom.

The thought sent shudders through her.

"Bonnie?" Whit's voice startled her, and she trembled.

His arm went around her, but he quickly pulled it back. "Sorry. Are you ready to go inside?"

She nodded. It was better than telling an outright lie. Her heavy legs slowly moved up the steps and she felt anything but relief when she arrived at the top. Bonnie still had to walk through the door. The door where Angus had carried her across the threshold on their wedding day.

Her hands quickly went to her mouth. Had Whit planned to do the same thing? She couldn't hurt his feelings by denying him if he did, but it would mean nothing to her. She was certain it would be the same for Whit.

The door stood open, and her new husband caught up with her. He was breathless. Was that because he'd hurried to catch up with her, or was he overwhelmed by the entire experience like she was? More likely than not, he felt obligated to carry out the marriage ritual husbands had been doing for decades. It was meant to welcome the bride to their new home. Only for Bonnie it wasn't new. The memories she had here were bittersweet. She couldn't imagine making better memories with Whit. Or any memories, for that matter.

Bonnie was pulled out of her thoughts when she was lifted into Whit's arms. She glanced up at him, and into his handsome face. She blinked. Why was she even thinking that way? Bonnie had been coerced into marrying her husband's best friend. She hadn't wanted to marry again. And she certainly didn't want to come back to the ranch to live.

She sighed. Whit was right—she was unsafe in Wild Ridge. It had already been proven when she was abducted and held hostage at the saloon. The pungent smells of that room came flooding back and she swallowed. There wasn't a lot she remembered, but voices surrounded her, one in particular. Gus Jensen. It was that vile man who removed her clothes, she was certain of it. He force-fed her drugs to keep her compliant, except they made her ill. Bonnie would never get the memory out of her mind.

Tears ran down her face, and she closed her eyes against the world. Whit pulled her close against him. "Tell me. You must tell me what's wrong." His words were gentle yet urgent as he carried her into the house. When he put her down, it was on one of the sitting room chairs. When she opened her eyes again, he was kneeling in front of her. His hands held hers and his face seemed pained.

She sobbed, then tried to compose herself. "It was Gus. I remember his voice. He…." She couldn't bring herself to say the words. It was far too painful.

Whit cursed under his breath, but Bonnie still heard. It would take a long time for them both to get over what happened. The guilt Whit carried may take longer, despite her telling him repeatedly he had nothing to feel guilty about. She was not his problem. Except now he'd made her his problem.

For the rest of their lives.

Bonnie stood in the kitchen where she'd cooked so many times before. Only today she felt like a complete stranger there. Whit and Buck emptied the wagon of the supplies, and left them for her to put away, at her request. The pantry was near to bare, and hopefully Whit had purchased decent supplies for her to cook with. She'd been away for so long she had no idea how things worked around here anymore.

She stared out of the window toward her vegetable patch. It wasn't in perfect condition, but it was clear to Bonnie it had been cared for. Did Whit do that? He had never touched it when she lived here previously.

"A penny for your thoughts." Whit's voice got closer as he said the words.

She spun around to face him. "You looked after my vegetable patch. Thank you."

A small smile crossed his lips, but was gone as quickly as it had arrived. "I tried. I hope that was alright."

Alright? It made her heart happy. This way, they would have fresh vegetables to eat. She could make a stew, and even a roast. "Do we still feed the cowpokes, or do they look after themselves?" She didn't think to ask until now. It didn't bother her either way.

Whit studied her, and it took all her effort not to squirm under his gaze. "They've been coming in. Sometimes it was the only reason I got to eat a decent meal." He frowned then, and Bonnie wondered if he didn't mean to offer up so much information.

"I'm sorry I wasn't here for you," she told him, then turned away, staring out the window again. Bonnie was startled when his hands went to her arms.

"I didn't mean to imply…"

"I know." Bonnie turned to face him again. Whit stared down into her face, and she knew, in any other circumstances, things could be different between them. Only the one thing that stood firmly between her and Whit was her dead husband. It would never be any other way. It meant they would never have a real marriage, never have children, and they would never feel the love a husband and wife should have.

The revelation had her heart pounding. She had to get away from Whit, away from his warmth, and away from everything he stood for—including their fake marriage. Bonnie wondered if he'd shared her abduction with Buck. She shuddered at the thought, but knew for her safety that would be the case.

It meant the other workers also knew. Or at least they would in due course. She wanted to melt into the floorboards. Slink away where no one knew her, except Bonnie knew that was far too dangerous. Now that Gus Jensen had his sights on her, he likely wouldn't give up. Out here, far from town, he was less likely to come after her.

Did that mean she could never go into town alone? It was not a good idea, and she knew it. The thought of always having a man protect her sent shock waves down her spine.

Bonnie pushed past Whit, the contact sending tremors through her entire body. "I need to get these supplies put away."

His expression told her he'd felt it too. Her heart shattered. What would Angus say about all this?

Chapter Five

Whit longed to pull Bonnie close. Every time he looked at her his heart fluttered. He'd missed her so much since she'd moved to Wild Ridge. Refusing to stay at the ranch after Angus died had been the right decision. Although she was a widow, people would still talk.

He didn't care what people said, but Bonnie did, and that's what mattered. His heart broke the day he'd left her at the boarding house. Until that point, they'd only been friends, not through any fault of his own.

Except it was his fault. All those years ago, he hadn't fought for her. Angus claimed Bonnie and that was the end of it. If he'd pushed his way in, made his feelings known, his life might be different now. Would there be a brood of children running about? Whit glanced about. He could almost imagine their young offspring in the kitchen. Could hear their voices. It warmed his heart.

He shook his head to pull himself out of his stupor. It would never happen now. Not when they were to have a loveless marriage. One of convenience. Whit was certain that's what Bonnie would want, but hadn't discussed it with her.

He'd taken her belongings into the room she'd shared with Angus, but she'd been busy in the kitchen. He could help her unpack later if she wanted. But knowing Bonnie, she preferred to be independent. Wasn't that the reason she moved into Wild Ridge and got a job at the mercantile? So she didn't have to rely on him to survive? She'd as much as told him so.

He had begun to turn away when he saw her pick up a sack of flour. At least she tried to pick it up. "What are you doing?" he demanded. "Let me do that."

"I can do it myself," she said, a frown on her face.

He stepped toward her as the weight of it forced her to bend over. "Bonnie, let me," he said firmly. She nodded, but he knew it wasn't what she wanted.

"I forgot. We're married now."

Whit wasn't sure what that meant, but her words brought him back to reality. They were married and yet they were not true husband and wife. Whit wasn't certain he was ready for the reality of the rest of their lives.

Reality meant knowing Bonnie was his wife, yet he couldn't treat her like a wife. He easily carried the sack of flour to the pantry, then returned to find her stretching her back. She was beyond stubborn. Always had been. "Anything else you need taken in?" She smiled at him, and Whit's heart fluttered.

This whole marriage thing hadn't been a good idea, but it was the only solution to keeping her safe. If the sheriff had done his job, Jensen would have been locked up long ago, but the man was in Jensen's pocket. Whit was certain of it.

"It's too late to make a stew or even a roast for supper. Do you think the men would mind if I made pancakes with onion and potatoes?" She stared at him, her expression one he'd seen a hundred times before, and had dearly missed.

"They will be grateful for anything. We've taken turns cooking each night. The results have not always been good." He screwed up his face, and she laughed. He loved when Bonnie laughed—the sound always made his heart fill with joy. Oh, how he'd missed her.

"It's settled then. That's what we're having for supper. I'll whip up something for dessert. Perhaps an apple pie?" She pierced him with her eyes. "You do have apples, don't you?"

"They're amongst the supplies we brought home today." She smiled and his heart flip-flopped. Whit felt like he was a teenager again. He needed to reel in his emotions. During their marriage ceremony, it seemed like he was betraying his best friend. What he did was solely to honor his promise to Angus. More than anything, he had to keep Bonnie safe.

"Apple pie it is then," she said, then hurried into the pantry again.

Whit heard her rummaging through the small room, and it reminded him of days gone by. Memories of the three of them, living like a family, and both loving Bonnie. Not even once did he tell Bonnie how he felt about her. Not since Angus claimed her as his own, anyway.

Before Angus arrived, they were close. Whit was certain he would marry Bonnie. But it wasn't to be.

"Are you still standing there?" Bonnie said firmly. "I can find plenty for you to do." She chuckled, and so many memories flooded his mind. It was not what he wanted, nor was it what he expected. They'd been apart for so long now—almost since the day Angus had died. He'd kept an eye on her, making sure she was doing okay, even if it was from a distance. Occasionally he'd speak to her at the mercantile when he went into town for supplies, but that was it.

Now Whit wished he'd insisted she stay here. Insisting she marry him back then was probably a better option, but she was mourning. He didn't want to force that on her.

He stared into her face. She had been reluctant to come inside, he could tell. There were too many memories here for Bonnie as well. Most of them happy. Right now, she was far from happy. Whit dearly wanted that to change.

"Whatever you need," he said. He'd already lost close to a week. He'd lost count of the days he'd spent at the doctor's office, worrying about her. One more day was not going to hurt. Buck always kept the place running as it should. For that, Whit was truly grateful.

She smiled again. Oh, how he'd missed that. It had been far too long since Bonnie had graced his kitchen and his home. "If you could carry the heavy bags into the pantry that would help. Is there much in the root cellar?"

He hadn't given it a lot of thought. "There's bits and pieces. Sorry, I really can't remember. I can come down with you if you like." Whit could have kicked himself. Their root cellar wasn't large. You could barely fit two people in there, and even then you were at close proximity to each other. He shook himself mentally. What a stupid thing to say.

"I'd like that." It was then he realized she was likely still on edge. Jensen and the sheriff had a lot to answer for. Whit felt his anger rising again, and tried to control it. He wasn't a man to lose his temper often, working as a bounty hunter taught him that, but when it came to those two… "Can we do that now?" Her voice calmed him. It always had.

Bonnie reached out and took his hand, giving Whit no choice but to follow her to the root cellar.

Absolute dread filled him.

Chapter Six

Bonnie slowly descended the steps to the root cellar. She'd always hated going there, but today was worse. Those awful memories plagued her.

She'd been in there, rummaging for something to cook for supper when Whit had called her back up. Angus was dead, he'd told her.

At the time, it was the worst day of her life. The day she was kidnapped had surpassed that. Bonnie knew exactly what her fate would be in the hands of Gus Jensen. And suddenly, although it broke her heart, Angus's death took a back seat.

She held tightly to the rails on either side of the steps. Whit was right behind her, and while that was in some ways comforting, there was limited space for the two of them to move about.

Her feet finally hit the ground, and she moved across to let Whit in. She glanced across the shelves, only to discover it was poorly stocked. "How long has it been since you've restocked it?" she asked, realizing it could have been months. Or perhaps longer. Since she left even.

Whit stared at her. "No idea. It's a long time, I know." He shrugged his shoulders and Bonnie decided it hadn't been easy for him all this time without a woman to help run the ranch house. There was no sign he'd had a housekeeper, so assumed there was none. He was a man of habit, always had been, and a housekeeper likely wouldn't fit his sensibility.

But a wife would.

Besides, he didn't trust easily. Spending time as a bounty hunter taught him that. Bonnie had hated that part of his life, and Whit never talked about it. He refused to tell her if he'd ever killed a man, or if he'd been shot. It wasn't suitable for her precious ears, he'd always said. If it hadn't got her back up, it would have been laughable.

Bonnie's eyes zoned in on a bucket. The closer she got, the worse the smell. It was overpowering. "Oh!" she said as she backed off. "That's disgusting. How could you leave milk down here for so long? The smell is foul." She was certain she would heave if she stood near it. Whit reached over and took the offending item away.

"Anything else?" he asked, a sheepish look on his face.

"You tell me," Bonnie said firmly as she shook her head. "I can see I've got a big job ahead of me." She sighed, but knew it would fill in some time, and likely keep her sane. Not that she had ever been bored on the ranch. There was always plenty to do.

Whit reached across in front of her, and lifted a decidedly moldy loaf of bread. He rolled his eyes. "That's likely left after…" He stopped abruptly, and Bonnie was curious about the reason. She studied him. "After the wake," he whispered.

"No wonder it's moldy! It needs to go, too." Her eyes scanned the remaining items. There were a few potatoes, some carrots, and beets. "I'll use those up before the fresh vegetables from the garden. How old is the salted meat?"

"A few months at most," Whit said. "It should be fine."

Bonnie stepped closer to get a better look. Bumping into Whit on her way was not her plan. The less contact they had, the better. With the root cellar being so narrow, it was near impossible to get past without touching each other.

Whit stared down into her face. She endeavored to move past without touching him, she really did, but it wasn't to be. Bonnie felt his warm breath on her face. It was the only warmth down here. She had forgotten how cold it got, and should have grabbed her shawl. Only it was still packed. Somewhere. She had no idea where her belongings ended up.

Turning her face away, Bonnie suddenly felt the full impact of being down here. The cold, the memories, being so close to her now husband. She shivered.

Then she shuddered. So many feelings hit her all at once.

She wanted nothing more than to be held in Whit's arms. Instead, she headed for the steps. It wasn't easy to hurry up them. They were steep, not to mention the long length and bulk of her skirts. At least she was empty-handed.

"Bonnie?" Whit's voice followed her, but she couldn't stop. Once at the top, she ran outside. Fresh air was what she needed. Whit's heavy footsteps followed, and she knew it was inevitable he would catch up with her. He was a good foot taller and his legs far longer. "Bonnie," he said again when he'd caught up. "Tell me what's wrong." He opened his arms and she was sorely tempted. Her heart pounded, but she was confused.

Slipping into Whit's comforting arms would feel good, but what about Angus? How would he feel about this entire situation?

"Bonnie, I want to help," Whit said, then stepped forward and enveloped her in his arms. It felt far too good.

She closed her eyes and leaned into him. It was nice. She felt completely cocooned and protected. Nothing bad could happen to her with Whit by her side. He was right to insist she come back to the ranch to live—Bonnie should have done it long ago. She understood why he'd insisted they marry. She wouldn't have agreed to coming back unless they were man and wife.

As far out from town as they were, tongues would still wag.

She sighed, then opened her eyes. The fresh air had done her good. Bonnie rolled her eyes. It wasn't the fresh air, but Whit's comforting arms that had helped. "Thank you," she whispered. "I needed that."

He stared down at her. "Truth be told, so did I," he said quietly.

They were similar, always had been. Angus's death had rocked them both, but instead of being there for Whit, she'd run. Bonnie had regretted it almost from the moment Whit had left her at the boarding house. She'd gone to her room and cried a river of tears, not only for her lost husband, but for the best friend she'd always had.

Now they were reunited, but life would never be the same. Bonnie was still young and of a child-bearing age. She wanted babies. Lots of them. But had no idea what Whit had planned for the two of them.

"Whit," she said, staring up into his face. "We need to talk."

~*~

Bonnie poured coffee for Whit and tea for herself. There were fresh cookies in the pantry—they'd arrived in today's supplies. Once they were gone, she would bake her own. Not that the mercantile cookies were terrible. They weren't. She'd eaten her fair share of them while she worked there.

Whit sat at the table watching her every move. He seemed on edge, and had every right to be. Telling him she wanted to talk without giving him a reason was unfair. She could see that now.

After placing a mug of coffee in front of him, strong and black, she sat down and reached for one of the mixed cookies. Except she had no appetite for it. Apparently neither did Whit—he held one in his hand, but hadn't eaten any of it.

"What are we talking about?" he asked quietly. Had he guessed the topic of conversation? Or perhaps he was concerned about what it might be.

Her mouth was suddenly dry. She took a sip of tea and let it slide down her throat. It only helped a little. "We should discuss our marriage," Bonnie said, not giving anything away.

Whit swallowed. What had he expected her to say? She wasn't going back to town if that's what he was thinking. "I won't agree to an annulment," he said firmly. "So don't even ask."

Bonnie shook her head. "I…that's not what this is about. I want to know what you expect from our marriage. We both know there's a wall between us."

Picking up his coffee, Whit took a long sip. "Angus," he finally said.

That one word said it all and they both knew it. She swallowed back the emotion that one word evoked. For her it was heartache. "I know you only married me to keep me safe. It's not a secret. But I need to know what you expect from me in return." Bonnie was being as straightforward as she could, trying not to become emotional. She was being pulled in so many directions by her heart and her memories, she was far too confused.

"What do *you* want from this marriage?" Whit was putting it all in her hands, and that wasn't what she wanted. Bonnie simply needed to know where she stood.

"I will be your cook and housekeeper. I assume that was your plan."

Whit looked down at the cookie he'd held for so long and shoved it in his mouth. Did that mean he didn't want to answer? He'd have to swallow it sometime.

"I need to know where I stand," she said firmly.

Whit's eyes met hers, and he drank down the rest of his coffee. "You're my wife, Bonnie," he said quietly but firmly, then stood. "I need to check on the men. I'll be back for supper, along with the rest of the men."

He strode out of the room and was gone before she had a chance to respond.

Chapter Seven

Almost the moment he was outside, Whit breathed a huge sigh of relief. It was stifling inside.

Not really, but it felt that way. Especially in the root cellar. Why he'd agreed to go down there with Bonnie, he would never know. Doing so was tempting fate. While she was pressed up against him as she pushed past, he longed to wrap his arms around her. When he glanced down at her face, her lips were calling out to him.

Still, he managed to get out of there relatively unscathed. When she later asked his intentions about their marriage, he didn't know what to say. Instead, he got out of there as quickly as was humanly possible.

Now his heart pounded and his head hurt. Which was probably far better than the way Bonnie would have fared. No doubt her heart hurt right about now. They had been friends for far too long to treat her that way and Whit knew it.

Should he go back inside? If he did, what was he meant to say? Hand on the door handle, he stood frozen to the spot. Nothing had gone right today. He should never have forced her into marriage like that.

Surely people would understand after what happened?

He shook his head. No one in town knew what happened. If they did, surely they would have gone to the sheriff.

Whit dropped his hand from the door as though it had burned him. Now *his* heart hurt. His confusion threatened to overtake him at any moment. He loved Bonnie, always had. So what was the issue? All he had to do was open his mouth and say the words.

Except Angus's voice haunted him. *Keep Bonnie safe*, is what he said. Not *Marry my wife and make her your own.*

As he stormed down the steps, Whit didn't look back. He'd made a mistake bringing Bonnie here. A huge mistake, and one that could never be fixed.

"Why don't you go home to your wife?" Buck demanded. "You're like a bear with a sore head."

He was, Whit knew he was, but if there was a choice between working and spending time with Bonnie, knowing she wasn't in reach, he'd rather be out here in the fresh air. "I'm not that bad," he snapped. It was then he understood Buck's words were true. He closed his eyes and silently counted to ten. When he opened them again, Buck was staring at him.

The foreman slapped him on the back. "You still haven't told me why you married Bonnie. She was living happily in town. At least that's what you told me." He studied Whit, but said no more.

"It's like this," Whit said. "Gus Jensen kidnapped and drugged her." His voice began to waver, and Whit knew he had to quit talking or he would break down. It was the last thing he wanted to do. Especially in front of his foreman. "That's why…" He shook his head trying to shake away the memory. "It's the reason I was gone so long. She's been out cold in the doctor's office."

The other man cursed out loud. "No wonder you're on edge." Whit felt like he was under a microscope, Buck studied him for so long. Without warning, Buck slapped his leg. The sound startled Whit. "Angus would approve," he said firmly. "You know he would."

"Would he? I'm not convinced." Shaking his head seemed to have become second nature. It felt like all he'd done today.

Buck reached for his canteen and took a long drink. "Go home. Talk to your wife, clear the air. Do whatever it takes. You've waited a long time for this."

He had waited a long time, but this was not the way he wanted to win Bonnie over. It wasn't as though he'd won her affections. Far from it. All he'd done was convince her to marry him in order to stay safe. "It's a marriage of convenience," he blurted without thinking.

Buck dragged his Stetson off his head and ran a hand through his hair. "Then you're a bigger fool than I thought." He turned away then, the conversation effectively ended.

What he should do now, Whit wasn't sure. He did know where he needed to be, and it wasn't here with an ornery cowboy who would tell him the truth, no matter how much it hurt.

Whistling for his horse, Whit knew he had to head for home. Perhaps it was time to sit down with Bonnie and tell her the truth.

When he arrived back home, Bonnie was sitting on the porch swing, a mug in her hand. Whit dismounted from his horse, waved to her, and led the horse into the barn.

He'd give him a good rub down and feed him some oats, then sit himself down next to Bonnie. His wife.

It still hadn't completely sunk in they were married. And despite what Buck had told him, Whit wasn't certain Angus would be happy about him stealing Bonnie and making her his wife. He would love to hear Bonnie's thoughts on the subject, but wasn't sure if he should broach it. Especially today.

A lot had happened over the past days. Most of it because of Gus Jensen. The man was a pest to society and should be locked up. Of course you'd need a real sheriff for that to happen—one who wasn't in the saloon owner's pocket.

As he rubbed Rusty down, the horse seemed to know his mind was elsewhere. He nudged Whit a few times, and whinnied as well. It was not something he normally did. "I know, boy," Whit said. "I'll sort it out, I promise."

But making a promise to his horse, and keeping it, was far different from making a promise to himself. Or to Bonnie. After all, she was the most important person in this equation. Everything he'd done was to help her, to save her from Jensen.

When he'd brushed Rusty far more than he normally did, Whit fed the horse, then strode out of the barn. Perhaps Bonnie would be inside by now, and he wouldn't have to sit next to her.

He shook himself mentally. Buck was right—he had to stop running from the truth and tell Bonnie everything. As he climbed the steps to the porch, he noticed her still sitting on the swing. She leaned down and placed her mug on a side table. "Would you like coffee?" she asked, then began to stand.

"Stay there," Whit said. Since he'd had to work up the courage to do this, he couldn't put it off any longer. It seemed to take a lifetime to walk to the other end of the porch and join her. He sat down and his large frame filled the remainder of the wooden swing. It reminded him of the day he and Angus had built it, then hung the swing in this very spot. Bonnie had made them both sit in it to ensure it could take their weight. If it didn't, they would have looked like fools. Thankfully, it passed the test. "We need to talk," he said without looking at her.

Bonnie's intake of breath took him aback. Her hand on his knee startled him at first, but he covered her hand, and it felt good. "What do you think I tried to do earlier?" she whispered, and Whit knew she was right. He had stormed out before that could even happen. He was a fool. Not only for leaving when he should have answered her question, but for pushing her into marriage without telling her his plans.

Whit stared down at their entwined hands. It was a start he supposed. Even in a marriage of convenience it was permissible to hold hands. Surely.

He glanced sideways to find her staring at him, her expression one of expectation. It seemed he needed to speak first. "I thought…" This was harder than he'd anticipated. "I was planning on a marriage of convenience." There. He'd said it and that's all there was to it.

Tears filled her eyes, but Bonnie said not a word. She turned her head away, then wiped at her cheeks. He'd made her cry, and it shattered his heart. Whit reached over and held her chin gently, then turned her to face him. Her big brown eyes seared his, and Whit wanted the earth to open up and swallow him. He wiped at the tears that continued to fall down her cheeks. Bonnie opened her mouth to speak. "No."

That one word made his heart thud.

Chapter Eight

Whit stared at her in disbelief.

If he hadn't forced her to marry him, even though it was out of loyalty of his promise to Angus, they wouldn't be in this situation now. "Since you made me marry you, I expect a real marriage," she said firmly.

He stared into her face, then wiped her still flowing tears away. His eyes focused on her lips, and his thumb moved to caress them. Bonnie shuddered, and Whit's hand dropped to his lap. Had he taken that as a refusal? She'd already realized their marriage would be a difficult one, especially with Angus between them.

"I can't," Whit said, then stood. "What would Angus think?"

Bonnie stood too, then faced him. "Angus is dead." She'd had to face the fact and now it was time for Whit to do the same. "We're both getting on in age. We need to get on with our lives. You need a wife, and I need a husband. This will work in both our favors."

"We are married, so we've already achieved that," Whit said as he stared down into her face.

She felt the fury build up inside of her. "We might have a marriage license, but that's as far as it goes." Bonnie was so angry with Whit right now, she stormed off. Otherwise, she might regret something she said.

Her mind was swirling with what she needed to do next. It was obvious she couldn't go back to Wild Ridge to live. Gus Jensen would snatch her again, there was no doubt in Bonnie's mind about that.

Perhaps she could move to one of the outlying towns. Then again, if Jensen got wind of it, he would come looking for her. "Bonnie." Whit's voice wasn't far behind, but Bonnie wasn't certain she wanted to talk to him right now.

Regardless, she spun around to face him. "I thought we were going to talk," he said as he caught up with her.

"Ha!" she said. "You talk and I listen, right? I guess you get to make all the decisions." She took off again. This time, she headed outside. Perhaps if she pottered in the vegetable patch, she might feel more settled. Calmer.

Unfortunately, Whit followed her there.

Bonnie kneeled down and began checking the area. At least she knew there was food to be had from here. She pulled potatoes from the ground and sat them in a pile. It was all she could do not to throw them at her *husband*.

"I didn't know what else to do," Whit said. At least this time, he sounded genuine. His words sounded rehearsed earlier, as though he'd gone over and over them in his mind. "I promised Angus…"

"For goodness sakes," Bonnie yelled. "Can we leave my dead husband out of this?" Her impulses took over, and Bonnie threw a large potato at Whit. He caught it before it could do any harm.

"Bonnie," he said firmly as he frowned.

Embarrassment filled her. Normally she was far more controlled, but she was at her wit's end. Her husband reached out a hand and helped her to her feet. "Angus is gone," she whispered. "You and I are married. If you'd mentioned your plan for a marriage of convenience, I would not have agreed." She poked him in the chest. It was better than throwing a potato at him. Wasn't it?

She glanced up. His lips were pursed and his face taunt. She'd seen him like that before, and it never ended well.

Suddenly, his face softened. "It's all my fault." He ran a hand through his hair until it was sticking up every which way.

Bonnie chuckled.

Whit stared at her.

She began to laugh.

Whit's face screwed up. "What's so funny?" he asked, his hair still a mess.

She motioned for him to lean down. Bonnie ran her hands through his hair and put it back in place. Instead of straightening up, Whit stared into her eyes.

And then he kissed her.

~*~

Bonnie's breath was taken away. It wasn't like it was the first time he'd ever kissed her, because he had—many times.

The last time was several years ago—back when they were teenagers. Long before Angus came on the scene. As much as she'd loved Angus, Bonnie knew she still loved Whit, despite trying to deny her feelings for him.

She'd loved them both, but Bonnie had her heart set on marrying Whit. Then Angus had swooped in and claimed her as her own. From that moment onwards, Whit took a back seat.

It was of his own doing. She'd regretted that she'd allowed it to happen, right up until the day of her marriage to Angus.

It wasn't as though she was unhappy with Angus, because their marriage was deliriously happy. It was more about how her life would have been if she'd married Whit instead.

"Whitney Starkey, what do you think you're doing?" Bonnie had her hands on her hips and she stared at him. Instead of showing remorse, he grinned.

"You are my wife," he said, not an ounce of remorse in his voice. He kicked the dirt with his boot, and suddenly he was that teenage boy who had courted her all those years ago.

Whit was right. She was his wife, but only on paper. It was his choice to make it a loveless marriage, not hers. Bonnie had not agreed to any of that, and she'd made it very clear. "I don't understand. It's not that long since you said you only wanted a marriage of convenience. What's changed?"

"You've changed. Well, not you exactly. I can't really explain it." He stared down at the dirt and kicked at it again.

Bonnie couldn't help but smile. "I haven't changed in the short time since we sat on the porch." She kneeled down again and picked up the potatoes, holding them in her apron. Whit reached out a hand and helped Bonnie to her feet. As they touched skin-on-skin, she knew they could have a good life together if only they could get past her dead husband.

"I'll cook these with the pancakes for supper," Bonnie said, then headed inside. Whit followed, as she was sure he would. He was like a lovesick puppy, except a puppy didn't care about propriety or even the rules around newlyweds.

Being given a second chance was something she never thought would happen. Bonnie would prefer Angus was still alive, but since he wasn't, she would make the most of the situation they'd been faced with.

Chapter Nine

If the situation hadn't been so serious, Whit would have laughed. Since when did Bonnie throw vegetables at people. Or should that be at him specifically?

He'd confused her. Heck, he'd confused himself. Whit wasn't sure how long he could keep himself away from Bonnie, and the fact he'd kissed her had proven it. He hadn't planned to do it, but her big brown eyes drew him in, but when he glanced at her lips? They were calling out to him, and Whit couldn't help himself.

He placed the large potato Bonnie had aimed at him on the kitchen counter. It would never have connected, it was too far to the right. But that wasn't the point. That he'd riled her enough to think about throwing something, anything, at him bothered Whit. He had obviously upset her far more than he'd realized.

Bonnie dumped the remaining potatoes in the sink. Except some of them missed and fell to the floor and rolled away. Whit bent down to retrieve them. So did Bonnie. They almost collided.

"Sorry," Whit said, as he grabbed a few of the runaway vegetables. Bonnie also picked some up, but she was far more dainty in her movements than he was.

It was nice having a woman in the kitchen again. He shook himself mentally. What he really meant was he was ecstatic Bonnie was back home where she belonged. More than anything, he'd missed her. Sure, he'd missed her cooking, but it was more than that. He'd missed her sweet voice and her laughter. He couldn't explain it, even to himself, but Bonnie had been the center of his life, even though she was married to his best friend.

Whit should have moved out when they married. It would have been the best thing for all concerned. Even Buck had told him that, but Whit was far too pigheaded to listen. "I need water from the well," Bonnie told him, but her words didn't sink in. He was far too engrossed in his thoughts.

He was startled when Bonnie touched his cheek. "Oh, you are still alive," she said, laughter in her voice, then handed him the bucket.

Whit wasn't used to being bossed around by a woman. Not any more. It was something Bonnie had done when she was married to Angus. They were both told what to do in no uncertain terms. Neither one of them complained. Because they both loved her.

He strode out the door and went straight to the well. It wasn't far from the house, but too far for Bonnie to carry a bucket full of water. It was a rule they'd instigated when she and Angus had married. Bonnie was not to try and bring water in from the well. The one time she defied them, she had tripped on her way up the steps and landed on her back surrounded by water.

Her scream had brought him running out of the barn. Whit's heart pounded at the memory. He'd been so afraid of what might have happened. Snakes were not unheard of there, and he'd pictured her dying.

Instead, he couldn't stop laughing at the scene before him—Bonnie wet to the bone. Her hair stuck to her face, and her clothes saturated.

"Whit," she called from the porch. "What are you doing? Stop woolgathering—I need that water!" Her words made him smile. This was the Bonnie he knew and loved. Now all he had to do was move past the memory of her and Angus together.

Now it was Bonnie and Whit.

~*~

"That was delicious," Buck said, and the other men agreed. Bonnie had been a slave to the stove for hours, but not once had she complained. Whit knew the alternative was not palatable. Not for Bonnie, and not for his sensibility either. His heart hammered just thinking about her life right now if he hadn't discovered her missing in time.

Gus Jensen was an evil man. There was no other way to put it. One of these days, someone would put a bullet to his head. If necessary, that someone would be him. If he so much as came close to Bonnie again, Whit swore he would take care of the vile creature.

Bonnie stood and cleared the table. "Anyone for more coffee?" she asked, glancing around the table at their mugs. They all lifted their mugs. "I don't suppose anyone is interested in pie?" A smile lit up her face. Bonnie knew exactly what these men liked. She'd cooked for them so many times before.

Without waiting for an answer, she took the pie from the oven and cut it into slices, then served each man a large piece. Clotted cream was placed in the middle of the table for each one to help themselves. Bonnie refilled their mugs, then sat down at the table.

Whit reached for her hand under the table and squeezed her hand. Why he'd done that, he wasn't sure. They were married and he could do things like that if he wanted. Couldn't he? She glanced at him and smiled.

Happy sounds came from the men sitting around the table. They were more like family than workers, and it was good to see them happy. They had all endured a lot of awful cooking since Bonnie had left. Whit's included.

"We're glad you're back, Mrs. Starkey," Buck said between mouthfuls. Whit knew his words were double-edged. Not only was Buck happy to have her back here cooking for them, but he knew how unsafe Bonnie was in town. He prayed she was safe out here on the ranch.

Whit doused the fire in the sitting room as Bonnie came out of the bathroom. He glanced up and caught a glimpse of her in her flannel nightgown. She was a sight to behold. Bonnie wore her robe, but it wasn't tied and laid loose around her shapely body. How he longed to hold her, but more likely than not, Bonnie would not allow that. Despite it being their wedding night.

Besides, he'd put all her belongings in the room she'd shared with Angus. He mentally kicked himself for his stupidity.

When he glanced down, her feet were bare. She had beautiful feet, even if they were tiny. It set his heart racing. Whit couldn't believe his reaction to his wife. A woman he'd know for so long. A woman he'd longed for and had planned to marry.

Until Angus arrived in town.

And there it was. At every turn, the ghost of Angus McBryde was there. Now Bonnie had called him out on it, Whit desperately wanted a real marriage with her. How could that happen with Angus always looking over his shoulder? Even when he'd kissed her earlier today, he felt Angus watching.

Whit shuddered. There had to be a way to remove Angus from his thoughts and from their lives. As much as he'd loved Angus, he did not want him to dictate how the newly married couple lived.

He glanced up when he realized Bonnie was standing in front of him. "I'm going to bed," she told him. "Are you coming soon?"

Now he was confused. "I thought you would stay in the room…" He couldn't bring himself to say the words, *you shared with Angus*.

"Is that why my belongings were in there? No, I told you," she said without waiting for an answer. "It's a real marriage or no marriage at all."

Without another word, his barefooted wife trotted off to the bedroom they would share from now on. Whit scrambled to his feet and hurried after her. All thoughts of Angus hopefully pushed aside for the remainder of the night.

Chapter Ten

Bonnie awoke with a start. It was late, she could tell. She'd slept later than she had done for a very long time. Perhaps all those horrid drugs Gus Jensen had pumped into her had caused it.

She rolled over toward her husband, only he wasn't there. His side of the bed was cold. Bonnie jumped out of bed and reached for her robe. She had to make breakfast—the men would be looking to eat soon.

Now she panicked. What time was it?

She slid her slippers on her feet and opened the bedroom door. Laughter and murmuring met her and sent a cold shiver down her spine. She had one job to do, and that was feed the men. She'd messed up on her first day.

Bonnie couldn't help but feel like a failure. She'd always done her very best, no matter the endeavor. She'd messed up and wasn't sure how she could redeem herself. Closing the door as quietly as she could, Bonnie retreated into the bedroom and sat on the side of the comfortable bed contemplating her failure. How could she make it up to Whit and his men?

The door slowly opened and her husband stuck his head around it. "Good morning," he said as he grinned. Bonnie knew he was remembering last night. Heat came into her face and she wanted nothing more than to crawl under the covers.

"I... I'm sorry. I didn't mean to sleep in." She had far too much to do for that to happen. Whit had kept the ranch house tidy, but it needed a good clean. No doubt there was washing to do as well. Not to mention the meals she needed to prepare. Oh, and her clothes that needed to be brought into this bedroom.

Whit shrugged his shoulders. "Don't worry about it. We're used to getting our own breakfast. We have a routine," he said, then stepped toward her. Bonnie shivered. She was still getting used to Whit being her husband.

He pulled her up from the bed and wrapped Bonnie in his arms. "How are you feeling this morning?" Staring down into her face, Whit frowned. "Is something wrong?" he asked quietly. Had she shown her dismay at letting everyone down?

"My first full day here, and already I've failed everyone."

His arms tightened around her. "You definitely haven't failed anyone," he assured her. "We've been looking after ourselves from the moment you walked out that door. We will survive." He lifted her chin with his fingers, then leaned in and kissed her gently. "I could get used to this," Whit said, but Bonnie knew he was holding back.

When the kiss was over, she rested her head against his chest. Bonnie felt comforted when he held her. So much had happened recently, and she never wanted to experience that terror again. No matter she was drugged, Bonnie heard every word said in her presence, and felt everything that was done to her. Thankfully, the worst thing to happen was Gus Jensen undressing her. The filth that came out of his mouth shortly afterwards was something she would never forget.

She was totally helpless, and was convinced she was there forever more. Bonnie fully expected one of Jensen's *clients* to visit her room to ensure she never left. She was grateful that didn't happen. It seemed his clients had far more morals than the saloon owner would ever possess.

Bonnie shuddered, panic vibrating through her entire body. She pulled back, trying to free herself from Whit's hold. Her heart thudded and she felt lightheaded. "It's alright," Whit whispered. "I've got you." His soothing words helped to calm her, and his arms wrapped around her again. "The doc told me this might happen. Did you remember something?"

She nodded against his chest. "Gus Jensen undressing me." Her breath caught in her throat, and Whit swore out loud. She didn't chastise him as she might normally do. If she was him, Bonnie would swear too.

It was too unladylike for her to do so. At least that's what her mother always told her. "Aw, stuff it," Bonnie said, then added a few choice swear words of her own.

"Bonnie Starkey," Whit said, his voice a cross between condemnation and laughter. "I didn't know you had it in you." He raised his eyebrows at her.

"I believe the occasion called for it," she said, and fully believed that was the case. She didn't want to move from holding onto Whit. Bonnie would have happily stayed there all day. "I assume you are going back to work today," she asked, her sadness clear in her voice.

He frowned as he glanced down at her. "Would you rather I didn't?"

She would prefer he never left her side. No longer was Bonnie the carefree woman she once was. After her dreadful experience, she'd been left a shell of her former self. She was not trusting of anyone she didn't know, and she was afraid to be left alone. Except she couldn't tell her husband. He had to earn a living, and that meant working on the ranch, along with the other men.

"You can't stay home. You have a job to do. Besides," she said firmly, "I have a lot to do today, and you would only get in my way."

"Well, if that's the way you feel," he said with a chuckle in his voice, "I guess I have to leave soon."

Bonnie tensed. Telling her husband to go, and having the house completely to herself were two completely different things. Would she be safe? She silently cursed Gus Jensen for making her feel this way.

Bonnie went up on her tiptoes and kissed her husband's lips. "I'll be out shortly to clean up the kitchen," she said, then pushed him out the door of their bedroom. Whit joined the others in the kitchen, and soon quiet ensued.

She was completely alone, and Bonnie didn't like it one little bit.

Instead of making herself crazy with worry, Bonnie kept herself busy. First, she put on a roast for supper, and soup for lunch. Then she washed the dishes and tidied the kitchen. The floor could do with a wash, so she did that too. She'd even baked cookies.

The sun was in the sky, so she went into the laundry and found a basket full of washing. Mostly sheets. Bless his heart, Whit must have stripped the beds recently. It was an arduous task washing those sheets, but it had to be done. While the sun shined, the sheets would dry, so that was a plus. Bonnie promised herself to make washing an almost daily task, to keep on top of it.

With all that done, she was exhausted, and Bonnie made herself a cup of tea. The front porch was a lovely spot on a warm day, and memories of sitting there sipping tea in days gone by came flooding back. She reached for one of the oat cookies and took a bite. Lapping up the sun was something Bonnie could do all day. Except she had far too much to do.

She didn't blame Whit for the state of the house. After all, he had a ranch to run. Why he didn't get a housekeeper, for even one day a week, Bonnie wasn't sure. It couldn't be about the money. The ranch had always been prosperous.

Taking the last sip of her tea, Bonnie stood. She still had to make biscuits to go with the soup. It wouldn't be long and the men would arrive for lunch. Hurrying inside, she headed straight for the pantry to collect up the ingredients. It was then she heard the front door slam.

Chapter Eleven

"It sure smells good in here," Whit said under his breath. Then he glanced about. Where was Bonnie? His heart hammered in his chest. The place was quiet—far too quiet for his liking. He ran to the bedroom, but she wasn't there. As he headed outside to check if she was pottering with the vegetable patch, he heard movement in the pantry.

Praying he wouldn't need it, Whit had his hand on his gun. He moved quietly toward the pantry, and stopped when he saw his wife cowering in the corner. "Bonnie! It's alright." He opened his arms and she ran to him. Why hadn't he thought to announce his arrival? It was something he would be sure to do from now on. Her arms snaked around him, and Whit held her close. Bonnie was shaking uncontrollably, and he tried to console her. It was all his fault, and he needed to make it up to her. How he could do that, Whit had no idea.

He led her out to the sitting room and sat her on one of the chairs. Squatting down in front of her, he apologized, but knew it would do little to console her. "I don't know what I was thinking," he said quietly. And he didn't. He should have realized she would be afraid after her recent experience. Tears swam in her eyes, but Bonnie blinked them back. He wished she wouldn't do that. Releasing her fears and her anger was good for her.

Whit leaned forward and wrapped her in his arms. The shaking had mostly subsided, but was still noticeable as he held her. "Why don't you lay down for a while?" He already knew the answer, but it didn't stop him from suggesting it.

"I'm alright now," Bonnie said. "I have biscuits to make, and I have to stir the soup. I can't let it burn." She pushed him away and wiped at her eyes. Suddenly, she turned to face her husband. "Is that rifle still in the closet near the front door?" Her enquiring eyes studied him.

Whit came to a stand. "It's where it's always been. But I don't want you…"

She cut him off. "Is it loaded?"

Whit's heart pounded. "It's always loaded, but Bonnie, it's too dangerous for you to…"

Once again, she cut him off. "I know how to shoot. Angus taught me." It seemed like yesterday, but it was close to two years ago since she'd lost him, and even longer since she'd used a firearm of any sort.

Whit shook his head. This was far from a good idea. "Since you insist, let me give you a refresher," he told her.

"Thank you. It will have to be after lunch. I have biscuits to make and the men will be here soon." She shoved her way past him and headed back into the pantry.

Bonnie was always strong-willed. Whit was only now finding out exactly how tough she could be.

~*~

Whit was torn. He wanted to get back to work, but he didn't want to leave Bonnie alone again. Not after what happened earlier. She was in the process of cleaning the kitchen after lunch, and the men were on their way outside. Whit joined them but pulled Buck aside once they were on the porch. "Buck, wait up," he called as the workers made their way down the steps.

The foreman turned to face him. "Everything alright?"

"No. No, it's not. I have to give Bonnie a refresher on how to shoot." Buck's expression confirmed Whit's feelings about her using a firearm. "I know," Whit said before the other man had a chance to voice his opinion. "She'll do it with or without help, so it's better to ensure she knows what she's doing."

Buck nodded. "I agree." He turned to leave, then spun back to face Whit. "You don't think Jensen will come out here, do you?" His concern was clear in his expression.

"I wouldn't have thought so, but you never know with a man like that. He doesn't give up easily."

Buck rubbed a hand across his unshaven chin. "I need to alert the men. We have to keep your wife safe, and unless they are aware, they won't be on the lookout."

It had been Whit's hope to keep the information between himself and the foreman, but Buck was right. All his men needed to know the situation. "Go ahead," Whit said. "I'm heading back inside. No doubt Bonnie will push to have a shooting lesson today. We'll use the north paddock since you'll be working in the opposite direction."

Buck agreed. No point putting anyone in danger.

The two men parted ways and Whit made his way back inside. Bonnie stood at the sink finishing off the lunch dishes. "It's only me," he called, ensuring she wasn't startled again. She turned to face him.

His heart fluttered. She was incredibly beautiful, even with her soiled apron and her hair falling out at the sides. Bonnie smiled, then turned back to her work. Whit longed to hold her, but knew his interest wouldn't be appreciated while she had her hands in water. "Let me know when you are ready, and I'll take you for a refresher with the rifle."

Her nod was almost indecipherable, but Whit saw it. Her movements seemed to slow after that, but perhaps he imagined it. On the one hand, Bonnie was eager to arm herself. On the other, his recollection from years ago was she despised firearms of any description. He could see how that could be an ethical dilemma for his wife.

Bonnie had always had strong views. No matter the subject, she had her way of thinking, and there was no way to sway her. It was the reason Whit decided to humor her regarding the rifle that sat in the closet near the door. Angus had put it there the day they'd moved in. Added security, he'd said at the time. Not once had it been used.

The day he'd shown it to Bonnie, she had shuddered at the knowledge of a deadly weapon in the house. She accepted it was a necessity when living out here in isolation. That didn't mean she had to be happy about it, she told them at the time.

"I need to freshen up, then I'll be ready," she said, then left Whit standing in the middle of the kitchen.

He went outside and waited patiently on the porch. Whit breathed in the fresh air. It was part of the reason he loved it out here on the ranch. He enjoyed his work, and immersed himself in his surroundings. You didn't get that in the big city. Even the small towns like Wild Ridge didn't enjoy the same level of natural beauty he did.

"I'm ready," Bonnie said behind him.

Whit turned to find her clutching the rifle. The fully loaded rifle. He let out a long breath. One full of frustration. "Bonnie," he said firmly. "That firearm is loaded. Be careful."

She shuddered. Whit was not looking forward to this. Bonnie said she wanted it, yet he knew she really didn't. What she really needed, but couldn't have, was a bodyguard. Someone who would protect her day and night.

He wished that was possible.

Chapter Twelve

Bonnie took a deep breath. She hated firearms of any sort, but she now felt vulnerable. It wasn't something she liked or even coveted. She wanted the exact opposite. She had lived a relatively carefree life since moving to Wild Ridge. Until she'd noticed Gus Jensen watching her.

She would go so far as to say he was stalking her. Everywhere she went he was there. He'd even gone into the mercantile where she worked several times. In over a year since she'd begun working there, he had never been in the mercantile. He'd sent his staff, but not once had he personally shopped there.

That is, until he'd begun following her. Bonnie knew she should have told Whit, but she wasn't his problem. It was something she needed to sort out for herself. "I even told the sheriff," she muttered under her breath. It was too late by the time she understood she'd said it out loud.

"You told Sheriff Oakley that Jensen was stalking you?" Fists clenched, fury filled Whit's very being. "They both need a bullet to the head," he said, not attempting to cover his words.

"Whit!" Bonnie said firmly. "That is not a nice thing to say. Even if they are both evil." She shuddered again. Today was presenting many challenges, but she would win. She was not willing to lose.

He appeared a little calmer at her words, but now Bonnie worried Whit would go after the two men. "Promise me you won't do anything."

"I won't kill them if that's what you mean," he said, his irritation clear. "Those two are in cahoots. Something needs to be done. One without the other would not survive."

Bonnie knew Whit was right, but it didn't help the situation. He handed her the rifle he'd loaded moments ago, after unloading it before they'd stepped off the porch. *Safety first*, he'd told her, and Bonnie recalled Angus telling her the same thing. They were so alike, no wonder they were best friends.

"Tuck it in under your arm, and get comfortable with it."

Bonnie stared at him. How did you get comfortable with something so cumbersome? She tried despite her misgivings. Whit came up behind her and helped Bonnie with placement. His arm around her reassured Bonnie, but her husband wouldn't be there if she was alone and needed to defend herself.

His other hand placed her hand underneath to support the rifle, then he positioned her remaining hand on the trigger. She felt twisted into an unwieldy and completely unpleasant position.

"Aim at the empty cans, and pull the trigger," Whit told her gently.

Bonnie turned her head to study him. "I…I can't," she said. "You know I don't like guns."

"And yet, you sought this out," he said, sounding exasperated. She didn't blame him. Whit tightened his grip and forced her finger to pull the trigger. If he hadn't been behind her, Bonnie knew she would have fallen backwards from the recoil. "You don't have a lot of choice if you want to shoot someone." He raised his eyebrows at her, and Bonnie knew he was right.

"Apart from anything else," she said. "I wouldn't have time to get into position like this."

Whit took the rifle from her and stepped back before unloading it. "You're right," he said. "This is not working. Try this instead." He unloaded his revolver, then handed it to her. Bonnie stared down at it.

It sat across the palm of her hand. Bonnie did not move, she simply stared at it. Somehow, having an actual gun in her hand made it all seem very real. With her heart pounding in her chest, Bonnie wrapped her fingers around the handle. The Colt was big and it was heavy. For her, at least. She knew it was the firearm of choice for cowboys. Both Whit and Angus had one, and no doubt the other cowboys who worked here had a Colt as well.

Whit's hand wrapped around hers as she tried to get comfortable with the Colt. "Are you sure this is what you want?" he whispered, his voice unsteady.

She shook her head. "It's not," she said, her words wavering. "But I need to protect myself if Gus Jensen comes after me again." Bonnie stared up into his face. "He's the sort of man who won't let it go." Bonnie was convinced she was right.

Whit studied her, but didn't answer. They'd known each other a long time, and she'd always been able to read him. Today was different. She wasn't sure if he was only humoring her, or whether he agreed with her assessment. Either way, Bonnie wanted to be prepared if Jensen did breach Whit's property. She wouldn't always be surrounded by men who could protect her.

She knew Whit well, and was certain he would have made some sort of arrangements. At the very least, the cowpokes would have been apprised of the situation. Not that she wanted everyone aware of her business, but it was comforting to know they had her back.

"Do you want to give it a go?" Whit's voice cut through her thoughts, and it startled her. If her hand hadn't been wrapped up in his, she would likely have dropped his Colt. "It's alright if you'd rather not," he told her quietly.

A shudder went through her at the thought of Jensen coming after her. Before now it was all about protecting herself, but what if he truly did come out here? How had he managed to catch her off guard last time? Bonnie's memory had been vague on that, but her mind was beginning to clear. She wasn't sure that was a good thing.

An image formed in her mind of the day she was snatched.

Without thinking, she grabbed at Whit's shirt front. Whit took the Colt out of her hands. "What is it?" he asked urgently.

Bonnie was shaking uncontrollably. "I remember what happened. I'd left the boarding house to go to work. Out of the blue, I was confronted. Gus Jensen was there, along with two other men. Jensen sneered and shoved a hood over my head, and the other two grabbed my arms and legs then carried me to the saloon." The memory had tears rolling down her cheeks. She tightened her grip on his shirtfront. "What if they come here? I can't defend myself against three men."

Whit pulled a handkerchief from his pocket and wiped at her tears. Simply knowing he was there made Bonnie feel better, but it didn't help with her dilemma. His arms wrapped around her tightly and her head rested on his chest. Her tears made his shirt wet. but Whit didn't seem to care. Or if he did, he didn't mention it.

"We'll come up with a plan. Gus Jensen is an animal. He needs to be put down."

His words sent shock waves through her body. Whit was not a killer. Even as a bounty hunter, she didn't believe he would have killed a man for the bounty. He was not that sort of person. Except anger and revenge could change a man. And that was the last thing she wanted.

Chapter Thirteen

Whit was convinced Bonnie's fears were not unfounded, and yet, he couldn't tell her. Sheriff Oakley, in Wild Ridge, was in Jensen's pocket, so there was no point going to him. This would have to be handled here. There were enough men on his ranch to ensure Bonnie's safety. He didn't care if that meant she was shadowed everywhere she went. Even within the ranch house.

He already knew she would be furious, but it was too bad. Being a bounty hunter taught Whit a lot of things—especially that men could be wicked. Especially if it meant money in their pockets.

"I have a better idea," Whit said as he comforted his wife. He guided her back to the buggy, then packed up their makeshift targets. An idea was forming in his mind, but he was yet to work out the finer details.

One thing Whit knew, and that was he had no intention of leaving his wife alone again. Not now and not ever. After what had already occurred, he would have to be vigilant about protecting her. Being out here, where she was isolated from the town, Whit truly thought she would be safe.

Heck, he thought she would be safe in town. Jensen had other ideas. "It's all my fault," he muttered as he collected the cans. "I should never have let her leave the ranch." Except he knew Bonnie had no intention of living there with an unmarried man. It would be scandalous. To her mind, at least.

Why he didn't have the foresight to marry her straight away, Whit didn't know. Except he did. Marrying his childhood sweetheart right after her husband had been killed would set tongues wagging even more than if she'd stayed.

Fury built up inside him. Whit didn't get angry often. As a bounty hunter, he'd learned to curb his temper—it did him no good. He swore under his breath. This entire situation needed action. There was no way he could provide surveillance twenty-four hours a day. Although it was needed.

He also had a business to run, but Bonnie's safety must come first. He finished packing everything into the buggy, and climbed up next to his wife and pulled her close. She was miserable, but Whit had no control over the people who caused her misery.

Except he did. Whit knew exactly what he needed to do.

~*~

The trip into Green Valley took longer than it would to Wild Ridge. Whit knew taking the time to go to the outlying town was the better option. Gus Jensen didn't control the lawmen in Green Valley like he did in Wild Ridge. Sheriff Bartley was as clean as they came. As he sat opposite the man Whit admired, they came up with a plan, then headed to the telegraph office.

Money was no option, and Whit ensured Sheriff Bartley understood that was the case. Instead of returning to the sheriff's office, they headed to the diner when their business at the telegraph office was done. After they'd eaten, Whit would return home. Buck was guarding Bonnie, but it was something Whit preferred to do himself.

It wasn't that he didn't trust Buck—he trusted the foreman with his life. And his wife's life. Whit preferred to watch over Bonnie himself. Even if she didn't want him to.

She was tough, there was no doubting that. But she was also frightened, and Whit didn't blame her one iota.

He couldn't wait to get back home to Bonnie and hold her in his arms. To see for himself she was still at the ranch, still in one piece, was all it would take to put his mind at ease.

Soon everything would change. Whit was not going to sit back and let Gus Jensen kidnap his wife again. Nor did he want to see other women put in the same danger. Bonnie was far from the first woman Jensen had snatched—it was well-known where his soiled doves came from, and yet Sheriff Oakley did nothing. It's what convinced Whit the sheriff was on Jensen's payroll.

He planned to put an end to it.

Women needed to feel safe, be safe, going into Wild Ridge. Right now, they weren't. Bonnie could not return unaccompanied, even if she chose to do so, and that had to end. The plan he'd worked out with the sheriff of Green Valley was his only hope of eradicating the lawlessness going on in Wild Ridge.

As he pulled up outside the ranch house, Whit's heart fluttered. He sighted Bonnie as she glanced through the window, then disappeared. She stood at the open door before he even got up the few steps to the porch. They embraced as though they'd been apart for months rather than hours.

Why he'd ever believed a marriage of convenience would work, Whit had no idea. He loved Bonnie with all his heart, and would protect her with his life.

He whispered in Bonnie's ear, "I bought you a gift." She pulled back slightly in his arms.

"A gift? You didn't have…"

Whit interrupted her words. "I wanted to." He reached into his pocket and handed her the small package wrapped in brown paper and sealed with a ribbon. A smile broke out on her face, and it filled his heart with joy. "It's not much," he said. "But I knew you would like it."

Bonnie quickly opened her gift and dabbed the perfume onto her wrists, then breathed in the aroma. "It is superb," she declared, then kissed him. It was the first time he'd seen her genuinely smile for some time. If he thought perfume, or indeed other gifts, would restore her happiness, Whit would spend his entire fortune on her. Sadly, it was only a temporary fix. No matter if he filled the entire house with gifts, her troubles still lingered. Hopefully, his actions today would serve to eliminate the problems permanently.

"I have coffee ready, and blueberry muffins. They're not long out of the oven." Bonnie hurried to the kitchen before he even had a chance to respond. The ride had been a long one. More than that, it had been stressful, knowing the reason he'd gone. All the time, he'd wondered if Jensen would breach his ranch in his endeavor to retrieve his prize—Bonnie.

Whit's heart shattered thinking about it. If he hadn't discovered her missing, he knew exactly where she would be now, and what she would be enduring with no means of escape. He shook his head, trying to clear the image that was so vivid in his mind. Angus would never have allowed such a thing to happen. Of that, Whit was positive.

He would never forgive himself for what she'd been through, especially when he could have prevented it by insisting she stay and marry him after Angus's untimely death.

"What are you doing?" Bonnie's sweet voice asked. "Come and sit down. You too, Buck." The aroma of freshly baked muffins assaulted him, and Whit soon found his mind going to the delicacies he was about to eat. He needed a good distraction.

Things were in hand. Plans were afoot. Soon, Gus Jensen, Sheriff Warren Oakley, and all their cohorts would discover they were not as protected from the law as they thought they were.

"This is delicious," Whit said.

Buck agreed. "You've always been an excellent cook," he said right before he took another mouthful.

"I've missed being able to tinker in the kitchen," Bonnie confessed. "I am very happy to be back here where I belong." She was beaming, and Whit knew he'd done the right thing bringing her here. Now all he had to do was eliminate the threats that hung over her head.

Chapter Fourteen

As she sat eating a warm muffin, Bonnie studied her husband.

Before leaving, Whit wouldn't tell her why he was going into Green Valley, and she surely didn't need to know, but it piqued her curiosity. Did he want her to believe he'd gone all that way to purchase a gift for her?

She resisted the urge to roll her eyes.

If all he wanted to do was buy a gift, he could have traveled to Wild Ridge in far less time. No, that wasn't the reason, but he was being particularly secretive about his trip.

Now he was back, Whit did his best to let her think nothing was wrong. She knew him too well, and could tell something was on his mind. His entire demeanor bothered her. Whit was trying to give the impression of a man who was worry-free, but she knew otherwise.

Bonnie drank down the last of her tea, then glanced from one man to the other. "Have you both eaten enough? Otherwise, take what you want so I can clean up."

The men reached for another muffin and she grinned. Whit and Buck both loved their food, but then most men did. She hurried into the kitchen with her mug, the small plate her muffin had sat on, and the now empty larger plate. She filled the sink with soapy water and set about her task. After drying her hands on her apron, Bonnie turned to the stove. Although it was far from ready, the stew smelled divine. She gave it a stir, then turned back to dry the dishes that awaited her attention.

Glancing across at the dining table, Bonnie noticed Buck and Whit had their heads together. They spoke in a low voice. She heard nothing more than a quiet murmur. It made her wonder what they were discussing. She shook herself mentally. More likely than not, they were planning for someone to be here with her at all times. It's what Whit told Bonnie he would do.

Except this appeared to be more than that. Something seemed…not quite right. She stared across at the pair. Until Whit noticed her watching. Suddenly he sat up straight, then reached for his coffee. He seemed to mutter something to Buck from behind his mug.

Bonnie despised secrets. Especially if she was being kept in the dark about something that involved her. Even more so if it was to do with her being in danger.

It was on the tip of her tongue to demand to know what was going on. Until she thought the better of it. Best to let the men sort things out. She wasn't entirely useless, but they were the experts when it came to firearms. She'd already proven herself to be incapable of handling them.

She hurried over to the table to snatch up the remaining dishes. As she suspected, Whit's mug was empty. He had held it in front of his mouth as a way to hide whatever he was telling Buck.

Her heart pounded. The revelation meant her husband believed she was still in danger.

Whit reached out and pulled her close. "You smell lovely," he whispered, right before he dragged her onto his lap. He kissed her forehead gently, and she leaned into him. In his arms was her favorite place to be.

That didn't mean she trusted everything he said, because right now, Whit was keeping secrets. Bonnie desperately wanted to know what they were.

One thing Bonnie hadn't missed living in the boarding house, was washing sheets and towels. Thankfully, paying rent meant it became someone else's job. Now that she was back on the ranch where she belonged, it reverted back to being her responsibility.

With the sun shining and a nice breeze in the air, Bonnie placed the sheets on the rope used as a clothesline. There was nothing better than the feel of clean sheets beneath you while you slept.

"Here, let me help," Whit said. She eagerly let him, as they were large and cumbersome. "How are you feeling, Bonnie?" he asked.

Did he think she was ill? Bonnie frowned. "What do you mean? There's nothing wrong with me." His head bobbed up over the top of the sheets, but she could barely see him from the opposite side.

"I was making polite conversation," he said. Except Bonnie didn't believe him. It was now close to a week since Whit had traveled to Green Valley. He'd been on edge since then. Something was going on, but she still hadn't been able to work it out.

She was now at a point where she'd given up trying. Surely he would tell her if he wanted her to know?

With the wet washing now relegated to the clothesline, Bonnie set about going back inside and cleaning the house. She had almost reached the front door when she heard the sound of horses coming down the long drive. She stiffened.

Whit glanced in the direction of the ruckus and smiled. "It's the new men I hired."

Was that what he'd discussed with Buck? If that was the case, why hadn't he told her? Bonnie wasn't sure what to make of it. "Oh. Luckily, I have a roast on for tonight. There will be plenty to go around." She studied Whit momentarily. "Why didn't you tell me they'd be coming?"

"To be truthful," he said, looking anything but truthful, "I wasn't sure when they would arrive."

Although it sounded plausible, Bonnie still felt uneasy. It didn't sit right with her.

Whit walked over to the wagon the four men arrived in. He welcomed each of them before introducing them to Bonnie. "You've had a long trip," she said after the introductions. "I have coffee on the stove if you're interested." She didn't wait for an answer but went inside.

They stayed outside with Whit for a few minutes, then came into the kitchen accompanied by her husband. "Thank you, Mrs. Starkey," one man said before he sat down. "We won't give you any trouble, I promise." He glanced at each of the other men before settling into his coffee.

Bonnie added a plate of freshly baked pound cake to the center of the table, then excused herself. There was still plenty to do, and although she'd been back for a while, she was still trying to get the house in order.

Some of the rooms still bore a layer of dust, and she needed to strip the sheets from the room she shared with Angus. Bonnie already knew it would be heart wrenching, but it needed to be done.

She heard mutterings from the other end of the house, but couldn't make out what was said. They seemed like nice men, and should fit in with the other cowpokes nicely.

As Bonnie worked at removing the sheets from the bed, the chatter continued. Then it stopped, and she heard the front door close. She was finally alone. Whether that was a good thing, Bonnie wasn't sure. All she knew was she enjoyed the peace and quiet of living out here. Lately, she hadn't been afforded the luxury of being alone.

Until now, Whit had ensured there was always someone by her side. Finding herself completely alone was unnerving.

The question was, why was she suddenly left alone?

Chapter Fifteen

After removing their scant luggage, the man who'd introduced himself as Nick unhitched the wagon and followed Whit into the barn. He showed Nick where the tack was, and where to find feed for his horses. After Whit had helped the man brush down the horses, Whit led him to where he could store the wagon.

"I see your problem," Nick said. "Your property is huge. We can get the job done. Don't you worry."

Whit wasn't worried. He was told this team was the best for the job. They were met outside by the other three men—Daniel, Joe, and Ben. "Buck should be down shortly to show you your accommodations and give you a rundown of the property," he told them. As if by magic, Buck suddenly appeared.

Buck shook each man's hand as they were introduced. He seemed as happy to see them as Whit was. His hope was having them here would take some of the pressure from not only himself, but his workers as well.

"Supper is here at five," Whit told them, then headed back inside. Buck would look after them, and fill them in on everything they needed to know.

All he had to worry about now was ensuring Bonnie was happy and felt comfortable. He'd noticed how upset she'd been lately, and it bothered him. She wasn't sleeping well either. Whit felt for her, he really did, but wasn't sure what else he could do to keep her contented. The last thing he wanted was for her to run. He wouldn't put it past her—she'd tried to do that immediately after Angus had died. She'd eventually left, that was true, but he'd taken her into town himself when she'd insisted she couldn't stay. That way he was able to ensure she was settled and safe.

Little good it did. Jensen had bided his time until Bonnie's guard was down. That's the way the man worked.

Just thinking about Jensen made his stomach churn.

"Oh, you're here," Bonnie said. "I thought you'd gone with the others." She raised her eyebrows in question.

"I was in the barn, showing Nick around. I wasn't far." She stared at him. Bonnie seemed suspicious lately, Whit was certain of it, but she had nothing to fear. There were plenty of well-armed men on this property who would look out for her.

She strolled into the kitchen and opened the oven door. Using a kitchen towel to protect herself from burns, Bonnie basted the roast. She added potatoes and other vegetables to the fat, and closed the door again.

Whit breathed in the delicious aroma. "It's so good having you back here," he said, then stepped toward her. Bonnie stepped back.

"I'm pleased to be back," she said. "But I have a lot to do." She pushed her way past her husband and headed toward the pantry.

"Anything I can do to help?" Whit called after her.

"Highly unlikely," she called back, sticking her head around the corner. "Actually, yes, you can," she corrected. "Come in here and carry these into the kitchen for me." She filled his arms with apples, then collected milk, butter, and flour. "I'll come back for the rest," she told him. Then they headed out to the kitchen.

"Apple pie?" he asked after dispensing the apples onto the kitchen counter.

Bonnie stared at him momentarily. "How did you guess?" she asked, then chuckled. "Everyone loves apple pie. I'll have to make two this time. One pie won't be enough to go around." She was right, and Whit nodded his agreement. "I forgot the sugar. Would you mind grabbing it for me?"

He went straight to the pantry and went to hand it to her the moment he returned. Only Bonnie was staring out the window, toward her vegetable patch. "What are they doing out there?" she demanded.

Whit scratched his head. The four newcomers were wandering around the area at the back of the house where their vegetables grew. "Probably familiarizing themselves with the layout," he said. "What other reason would they have?"

"Are we certain they are not connected with Gus Jensen?" Bonnie asked quietly, her face suddenly pale.

Whit put an arm around her. "They definitely aren't. They were recommended by a friend who has used their services previously."

He heard his wife's sigh of relief. "See, they're already leaving. Buck probably sent them to familiarize themselves with the property." Whit pulled her close and wrapped Bonnie in his arms. "You're safe, I promise. There is no need for worry."

Bonnie nodded, and he held her close. He wasn't convinced she believed him, but there was nothing more he could do right now. He only knew she was well protected out here on the ranch.

~*~

"This meal is delicious, Mrs. Starkey," Nick said between bites. "I've not eaten this well for I don't know how long."

The murmurs of agreement didn't surprise Whit. "My wife is an excellent cook. You won't find one better," he added.

"I won't disagree with you," Buck said. "We missed Bonnie's cooking when she left." Whit glared at him, and Buck suddenly clammed up. It was a sore point with his wife. She didn't like to talk about her time in Wild Ridge, especially given the events of late.

Bonnie stood abruptly. Not that it was anything different to the norm, but she had picked at her meal and not finished it. She likely didn't realize Whit even noticed. Except he had, and it had him worried. She was losing weight. He could attribute that to both her concern for her safety, as well as not eating properly.

She collected her plate and scraped the remaining food into the bucket for the chickens. Then she opened the oven, ready to remove the apple pies. Whit jumped up from his chair to help her.

"Stay there," Bonnie said.

Whit ignored her. "I've finished eating. I'll get them for you." He'd done the same for the roasting dish, but it was far heavier. Much too heavy for Bonnie to move by herself.

He placed the two apple pies on the wooden board set up for that very reason, and breathed in the delicious aroma. How they'd survived without her exceptional cooking while Bonnie was gone, he'd never know. But survive they did. There was nothing fancy like apple pies, but they didn't do too badly.

Whit reached for the bowl of cream and placed it in the middle of the tables. They'd had to make a few allowances to include four additional men, and to that end, Whit had brought in another table. It was old and hadn't been used for years, but pushing it up against the existing table meant they could all eat together.

He hadn't spent much time with the new arrivals, but the glowing reviews he'd been given about their work was all he needed. Simply knowing they would be here was reassuring. Buck already seemed impressed with them.

"Are you happy with your accommodations?" Whit asked the group.

Daniel spoke up this time. "They're good. Better than most places we've stayed."

"Food's better too," Joe said, and winked at Bonnie.

She seemed a little depressed lately, and Whit didn't blame her. If Gus Jensen could be put out of business, he would be very happy. He was certain Bonnie would be far happier too.

Despite his reassurances she was safe, Bonnie didn't seem convinced.

Chapter Sixteen

Bonnie was confused. In all the time Angus and Whit had owned the ranch, they'd had the same number of cowpokes, not once deviating from that figure. Of course, with Angus gone, they were down one man, but Whit had secured four additional men, not one.

It had Bonnie scratching her head in confusion.

She glanced across at the combined tables. It was nice to be home again, and even nicer to be appreciated. She just wished it wasn't under such terrible circumstances. As she sliced the apple pie and dished it out, the men all talked between themselves. Whit stood near to her, and Bonnie didn't complain. She knew it was childish, but she always felt far safer when Whit was around. Truth be told she always had.

She loved Angus, of that there was no doubt. But her first husband was not a nurturing man. He would have protected her if the need had arisen, but Bonnie wasn't convinced Angus would have gone to the lengths Whit had.

A shiver ran down her spine at the thought of shooting another person, let alone killing them.

What had she been thinking, asking Whit to teach her to shoot?

"Are you alright?" Whit asked close to her ear.

She had hoped he hadn't seen her shudder. Sometimes her thoughts got away with her. It was the very reason Bonnie tried to keep busy. If her hands were busy, her mind should be, too. At least, that was her reckoning.

Whit's arms went around her, and Bonnie leaned back, relaxing into him. "I am now," she whispered, meaning every word. "I need to finish slicing this pie," she added.

Despite her words, Whit still held her close for long moments. He seemed reluctant to let her go, and Bonnie felt the same way. Except they couldn't stand that way much longer. She had to finish serving the meal to the workers. They probably needed coffee as well. Of that, she had little doubt.

She shimmied out of her husband's arms and went back to the job at hand. Whit snatched up two bowls and placed them in front of two men. That continued until all the pie had been distributed, then the pair sat down. Bonnie picked at her food—it was nothing new. She was far too distracted by the thought of Gus Jensen coming for her. It was the one thing Bonnie was certain about. The evil man never gave up once he started something.

Bonnie would rather die than find herself in his wicked hands again.

She stared down at the pie. It looked delicious, and Bonnie had no doubt it was. She was an excellent cook. It sounded vain, she knew, but it was the truth. Everyone told her so, and she believed them. There was no reason not to.

"This is delicious, Mrs. Starkey," Ben, one of the new workers, said. "You are an excellent cook." He then filled his mouth with food.

The others murmured their thanks as well. Bonnie could take their praise all day. It helped bring her out of her depressive mood.

It wasn't that the other men didn't praise her cooking, because they did. She'd wondered, on more than one occasion, if they were saying it to be polite. Especially given they'd spent such a long time fending for themselves. After that, anything would taste good.

"Thank you," Bonnie said. "Please, do call me Bonnie. Mrs…" She stumbled on her words. Bonnie was still getting used to being Whit's wife, and had almost said Mrs. McBryde. "Mrs. Starkey makes me feel old." She felt Whit's eyes on her. Had he realized her mistake? Her heart thudded. The last thing she wanted was to hurt her husband. He'd been so good to her, even after she'd married his best friend.

"It's all true," Whit told them all. "My wife is the best cook in the county." He lifted his mug of coffee and swallowed it down.

"Here, here," Buck said. Had he noticed her error? Not that she'd actually said the wrong name, but she'd stumbled. The man missed little, in her experience, so nothing would surprise her.

Bonnie stared down at her pie again. This time, she lifted a spoonful of the pie to her mouth. It sat there for long moments as she savored the flavor. Then she swallowed it down. The men were right—it was good. Except her stomach churned after eating it. She'd been like that for weeks. She blamed Gus Jensen for the issue. There was no way to know what drugs he'd filled her with, or how much. Doc Trantor guessed it could be laudanum, but had no way of knowing for sure.

Whit was staring at her, watching how much she ate. Without even looking at him, Bonnie knew he was. She took another mouthful and swallowed it down. His face relaxed somewhat.

Her stomach was in turmoil. Bonnie shoved her chair back and ran outside. Whit was right behind her. He was there when she emptied what little was in her stomach. He'd held her afterwards, and comforted her. He didn't admonish her at all, but sympathized instead.

Bonnie glanced up at him, her eyes swimming with unshed tears. "Eating makes me ill," she said quietly. "I think it's whatever Gus Jensen pumped into me."

Whit swore under his breath and stiffened. Then he pulled her closer. "We'll go see the doc tomorrow. He might have something to settle your stomach."

Bonnie nodded. That was a good idea. She knew she was losing weight—the clothes she'd worn for years were all too big for her. Not wanting to worry her husband, she hadn't told him. Instead of trying to fix the problem, she'd let it get to a point she was almost in dire circumstances. Whit already had enough to worry about without making things far worse.

Whit led her across to one of the porch chairs. "We'll sit here for a while. I'm sure the fresh air will do you good."

He was probably right. Bonnie had been busy trying to bring the house back to the state she liked to see it in. Whit had done his best to keep it clean and tidy, but he had a ranch to run. He couldn't take on the role of housekeeper as well. Nor would she want him to.

"I'm sorry," Bonnie whispered, then slunk down into her chair.

Whit stared at her. "You have nothing to be sorry about," he said firmly. "None of this is your fault. Breathe in the fresh air and try to relax." He reached across and held her hand. Bonnie liked it when Whit touched her. Being in his arms was the best feeling, and Bonnie never wanted it to stop.

"Except it feels like it's my fault," she said quietly. "If I'd listened to you and stayed here after Angus was killed, none of it would have happened." Her tears escaped and slid down her cheeks. Bonnie hated feeling weak, giving into the fears.

Whit wiped her tears away and leaned into her. "I won't have you talking like that," Whit said gently. "There is only one person to blame for all of this, and that's Gus Jensen. He..." His words stopped abruptly, and Bonnie wondered what her husband had been about to say. She suspected something was afoot, but couldn't figure out what. It was clear to her whatever it was, Whit didn't want her to know. Instead of continuing, he reached into his pocket and pulled out his handkerchief.

"I know it's not a fancy lace handkerchief," he said, smiling tentatively. "But this one can still wipe away tears." He gently wiped her face, then kissed Bonnie's forehead.

They sat together for what seemed like hours, not saying a word. It was all Bonnie needed. She didn't need words to feel comforted in Whit's presence. She simply needed to know he was there.

Chapter Seventeen

Whit felt bad about the stress Bonnie was under. Not to mention how upset she was. He truly wished she'd told him how bad she felt when she tried to eat—he could have taken her to be checked out far earlier.

It was then he realized she was probably avoiding going back to Wild Ridge, and who could blame her after what she'd experienced there? Whit would be with her every step of the way—there was no way he would allow Bonnie to go anywhere alone after her abduction by Gus Jensen.

Merely thinking about that man had his blood boiling, but Whit knew he had to keep calm for Bonnie's sake. He glanced across to see her rubbing at her arms. "Are you cold?" he asked, and she nodded in response. "We should probably go inside." Whit stood then and pulled Bonnie to her feet. Instead of taking her straight inside, he pulled her to him and wrapped her in his arms. She rested her head on his chest, and Whit savored the moment.

"Thank you," Bonnie said, glancing up at him.

Now he was confused. "For what?" There was nothing he could think of that he particularly needed thanking for.

She rested her head against him again. "For being there when I needed you."

He leaned in and kissed her gently on the lips. "Always," he said, then led her inside and out of the cold night air.

The workers had all left long ago, so it was the two of them alone. The moment they were inside, Bonnie reached for her shawl. The nights were cooler now, and Whit decided to light a fire. Bonnie headed straight for the kitchen.

"They cleaned up," she said, sounding incredulous.

"Good," Whit said. "That would have been Buck's doing. He's good like that. Always has been."

Bonnie stared at him as he squatted down at the fireplace. "I remember," she said. Then turned away and pottered about in the kitchen. Although what she had left to do, he couldn't be certain.

He added several twigs to the fire, trying to get it to catch. Whit added crumpled pages from an old newspaper, and set that alight. It looked more promising now.

It was then he heard the front door slam shut. His heart thudded.

Whit was on his feet and out the door in record time. What was Bonnie thinking, going outside by herself? What was she even doing out there?

He stood at the top of the porch steps and glanced about. It didn't take long to find her. Bonnie was at the well, pulling up some water. He hurried to her side. "Next time, wait for me. I don't want you out here alone," he said firmly. Moments later, a shiver went down his spine.

Someone was watching them.

Whit filled the large kettle with water, then carried it inside for Bonnie. If she needed water, she should have asked. It was especially important at this time of day, when the sun was low in the sky and the daylight was limited.

Anyone could be lurking about, and as it turned out, they were. Relief filled him the moment he spotted Nick and Joe in the shadows. At first, he was annoyed about the terror that had filled him. The moment he calmed down, Whit realized this was what he was paying them to do.

Keep watch and protect his wife. Nick tipped his hat at Whit from the shadows of the barn, where the two men were all but hidden.

"Next time, ask," he admonished once they were inside and alone again. "You don't know who is lurking outside." Even to his own ears, Whit's voice sounded strained.

She raised her eyebrows at him. "Like Nick and Joe, do you mean?"

Bonnie was far too clever for her own good. "If you saw them out there, I imagine they were out having a stroll."

"If that's what you want me to think, go ahead." Her words were filled with sarcasm. Not something Bonnie often did. Whit placed the filled kettle on the stove. Bonnie turned to her husband. "The stove needs more wood," she said tersely. "I'm going to bed." She turned away and headed toward the bedroom.

Whit knew he would have to tide things over, but wasn't sure how to explain his actions. Not that there was much to explain. His motivation was to protect her and ensure Gus Jensen got what was coming to him. Hopefully, his sheriff sidekick would be punished as well.

"Bonnie," he called after her, but she didn't answer. Instead, she slammed the bedroom door closed.

It wasn't often Bonnie lost her patience, or her temper, but it seemed he'd pushed her to the limit. The situation she found herself in likely wasn't helping. The slamming of the bedroom door was her way of telling him to find somewhere else to sleep.

Only Whit had no intention of sleeping anywhere except in his own bed.

He sat by the fire until he was happy with the way it burned, then filled the cookstove with wood. Whit dearly wanted coffee first thing in the morning. Perhaps by then his wife will have calmed down. Either way, Whit guessed he would have to explain.

Except he wasn't sure how to do that. He would have to talk to his new workers about being more discreet. To be fair, they surely didn't expect Bonnie to go outside in the semi-darkness, alone, to fetch water from the well.

He didn't either.

She'd certainly taken him by surprise. Bonnie was full of surprises—it was one of the things he'd always loved about her. Right now, though, it was the last thing he wanted her to do. Staying inside unless accompanied was imperative. Gus Jensen was evil. The man was as slippery as a slithering snake and would take any opportunity to grab his prize catch.

Despite the fact she wasn't his to claim.

Whit moved quietly toward the bedroom. The door was still closed. He hesitated, then quietly tapped on the door. No answer. Unsure if he should enter or leave his wife to sleep alone, Whit stood undecided for some time.

He tapped again, but still had no response. Gently, he opened the door and went inside. The room was in darkness except for the moonlight streaming through the window. Whit stood staring down at his wife. So beautiful and yet so vulnerable.

If it was the last thing he ever did, he would restore her faith in humanity. The best thing he could do to help Bonnie was to catch Gus Jensen in action.

Except he wasn't sure how to do that without putting his wife in imminent danger.

Chapter Eighteen

Bonnie murmured as she felt Whit's arms go up around her waist as she slept. Despite being annoyed with him, she was sorry she became cross with her wonderful husband. He truly was trying to help her, and she'd made his life miserable.

Truth be told, it wasn't her, but Gus Jensen who'd done that. Whit was yet another victim of the evil saloon owner. If Gus hadn't been so interested in her, Whit would not be in the situation he was in right now.

If it wasn't for the fact she was terrified, and admittedly vulnerable to the horrid man's plans, she would have left the ranch and applied for an annulment. Except she loved Whit and wanted to be with him for all eternity.

A tear slipped from her eye merely thinking about leaving him, and she wriggled trying to push her thoughts aside.

"Are you awake?" Whit's quiet voice cut through her thoughts. At first Bonnie didn't answer, but his hand gently ran down her arm. "I'm sorry," he said quietly. "I should have told you." He shuffled a little closer, and Bonnie reveled in his warmth.

His last words made her wonder what he should have told her. She now found herself in a dilemma. Did she tell her husband she was awake, or let him open up his heart to her. Perhaps disclosing secrets he wouldn't otherwise divulge?

"I brought them here to protect you," he said, his voice barely above a whisper.

Things were beginning to fall into place. "Are they marshals?" Bonnie asked as she rolled toward him. "Or simply hired guns who would kill Gus Jensen for you?"

The expression on his face was one of shock. Whit leaned in and kissed her forehead. "They're professionals. They are here to protect you, not to kill Jensen." He pulled her a little closer. "I'd rather see him rot in jail, along with his equally evil sheriff."

Bonnie nodded. This time, he leaned in and kissed her lips. At first, his kiss was ever so gentle, like the touch of a fairy's wings. The mood quickly changed, and Whit's kiss became frantic. Bonnie's arms went up around his neck, and she was pleased she had married the man she fell in love with all those years ago.

Not that she regretted marrying Angus, not even for a moment. Bonnie would never feel that way. She missed him dearly, but knew Angus would want her to move on. If she had to remarry, he would want her to marry Whit, his best friend. Not every man could be trusted, as had already been proven. Whit was trustworthy, she knew, even if he had gone behind her back.

Now reassured by her husband's intentions, Bonnie snuggled up close to him. "I believe you," she whispered. She closed her eyes, relaxing into his strong body. No matter where they were, being close to Whit always made her feel safe and protected.

When she awoke the next morning, it was to find her husband gone and the bed stone cold where he should have been. Bonnie glanced toward the window. The sun was shining through, telling her she'd slept in. Not for the first time since she arrived back to the place she loved so much.

She quickly dressed, then headed to the bathroom. Bonnie brushed her messed up hair and pulled it into place. Hurrying toward the kitchen, she heard the murmurs of the men. She'd let them down. Goodness knew what they were eating. Hardworking men like these needed a hearty breakfast.

Bonnie stood where the hallway met the kitchen and glanced across at the scene before her. Each man had a job. At least it appeared that way. Buck cooked the toast, Ben poured the coffee, and Whit dished out scrambled eggs to each man. It might not be what she would have prepared, but it would fill their bellies and tide them all over until lunch.

She cleared her throat. "Good morning, everyone," she said, announcing her arrival. Whit passed his job onto Joe and stepped toward her. His arms quickly surrounded her, and Bonnie leaned into him. "Why didn't you wake me?" Without waiting for an answer, she shrugged out of her husband's arms and headed into the kitchen. Everywhere she looked, there was a mess. At least they were fairly self-sufficient, and all she needed to do was clean up when they finished.

Once everyone had their food, she checked the large kettle. It still had plenty of water should the men decide to have more coffee before going off to carry out their chores. She glanced across at them and smiled. It was always good to see men enjoying their food.

At least for Bonnie it was.

She grabbed up a bucket and headed outside to the well, despite knowing she wasn't meant to do so.

When it was completely full of water, the bucket was too heavy for her to carry on her own. She would only half fill it and make two trips. Standing at the edge of the well, Bonnie began to wind the handle to bring up the fresh water she needed. She could have asked Whit—he would have helped—but she didn't need his help with this.

Winding the handle slowly, Bonnie stared down into the well. If she and Whit ever had children, she would ask him to make some sort of fence for the well, or perhaps a cover to ensure their children did not drown.

As she pulled the water up out of the well, she felt warmth behind her. "You didn't have to…" her words were stalled when a hand went around her mouth.

Bonnie's heart rate accelerated, but she knew she needed to slow it down. Otherwise she might faint, and she would be unable to alert the men to her dire situation. Calming herself so she could think clearly, Bonnie forced herself to relax. She had no idea who stood behind her, but it obviously wasn't her husband. Nor was it anyone who belonged on the ranch.

She lifted her leg as high as she could, given she was secured tightly around the waist. Her foot came down on her attacker's foot, and her mouth was released momentarily. That gave her the opportunity to let out an almighty scream before her mouth was covered again. This time, the attacker held her even tighter around the waist.

Things looked hopeless, and Bonnie was sure she was gone to Gus Jensen this time.

Chapter Nineteen

"Let the lady go, Jensen," Whit demanded, pistol in his hand. He didn't dare glance at Bonnie—he knew his heart would break. How he hadn't noticed her missing, he would never know. Except he did know.

He was too busy fraternizing with his workers. All of them.

One minute she was there, and the next Bonnie was gone. The moment he realized, he shoved back his chair—he knew exactly where she would be. Out at the blasted well. She was far too independent and would not ask for help. It was one thing to be strong, and quite another to be foolish. Especially given the current situation.

Her blood-curdling scream had him scrambling for the front door. He knew the others were right behind him, but wasn't sure exactly who was there. Whit couldn't afford to waste precious time worrying about that.

His hired guns would surely be there, too.

Gus Jensen seemed shocked at the situation he now found himself in. Out the corner of his eye, Whit noticed Wild Ridge's crooked sheriff making a run for it. Bonnie was his priority. The sheriff could wait.

"I'm not going to say it again, Jensen. Let the lady go or I will shoot." His words went unheeded, which truly frustrated and terrified Whit. Suddenly Bonnie stomped her boot hard onto Jensen's foot. His hands let go for mere seconds, but it was long enough for Bonnie to give him a clear shot.

Blood poured from Jensen's shoulder as he lay wounded on the ground. Buck ran toward the hardened criminal, while Whit ran toward his wife. He didn't check to see what else was happening around them. His sole focus right now was to ensure his wife was unharmed.

He wrapped her in his arms and held her close. Bonnie leaned into him. "I thought you were overreacting," she said quietly. "I believed Jensen had given up. At least I hoped he had."

Whit glanced down at her. Tears swam in her eyes, but she didn't let them fall. His heart beat furiously, and he could only imagine what her heart was doing. It must be going at a million miles an hour.

It was then he felt her sliding down his body. She'd taken him by surprise, but Whit's hands caught Bonnie before she hit the ground.

He carefully carried her inside.

~*~

Whit sat anxiously next to the bed, waiting for his wife to awaken. She had endured so much in the past months, least of all Angus's death. Now he wondered if Jensen was behind the murder. Had he been trying to secure Bonnie for his saloon all this time?

It had always been assumed cattle rustlers were behind the death. Now that he thought about it, the crooked sheriff was the one to make that suggestion. It made him more than happy to know his so-called hired guns had caught the dishonest sheriff trying to get away unseen. Except he was seen, and arrested on the spot. With Sheriff Nick Bartley amongst the newcomers, he was certain justice would be done. He was right.

With the three marshals by his side, they made a remarkable team of lawmen. They had been determined to stop Jensen, as well as his sheriff sidekick. Both would end up in jail for a very long time. That was if they had a lenient judge. If not, they would be hanged.

Justice in the west was often swift and harsh.

Bonnie's eyes finally opened and she glanced about. "What happened?" she asked in a whisper.

Whit squeezed the hand he'd been holding all this time. "You fainted," he answered, his voice low. Bringing her hand to his lips, he kissed it gently. "I was worried about you," he told her.

"Jensen?"

He knew what Bonnie was asking—would he continue to come after her. "He is locked up in Green Valley's jail, along with the former sheriff of Wild Ridge. They won't see daylight for a very long time."

"Former sheriff?" she asked, her voice incredulous.

Whit nodded. "He's been stripped of his position. He was here helping Jensen. Caught in the act, so no denying it." He couldn't help but sigh with relief. Finally, Bonnie's ordeal was over, and now they could live their lives without fear.

Bonnie nodded, then sat up. Whit watched her every move. She swayed, and he laid her back down again. "Rest up," he told her quietly. "I'll make you a cup of tea." He didn't wait for an answer, knowing she would refuse, but left her alone to ensure she rested.

He would never forgive himself for not noticing her disappearance, but at least now he could rest easy knowing Jensen would receive the punishment he deserved.

Sheriff Nick Bartley and the marshals were going to round up the rest of Jensen's henchmen, and ensure the women held unlawfully at the saloon were freed.

Whit couldn't be happier. This outcome was more

than he ever imagined.

~*~

Two months later, and life on the ranch was finally back to normal. It had taken Bonnie quite some time to believe she was free of the worry that Gus Jensen would come after her. From what Whit could tell, she had finally believed herself to be safe.

Sheriff Bartley and the marshals had testified at the recent court case, along with Bonnie. Whit had been right there by her side. It was a terrifying ordeal for her, having to recall her kidnapping. Doctor Robert Tantor was a key witness as well, recalling the details of Bonnie's state when Whit had found her.

Both men were found guilty and sentenced to be hanged in Helena two weeks later. Jensen's henchmen were jailed for ten years. It was the best outcome anyone could have wished for. With a new sheriff in Wild Ridge, and a new reputable saloon owner, the town was safe again.

As they lay in bed, wrapped in each other's arms, Whit knew Bonnie was his soulmate. She always had been, but he'd stepped back and let his best friend take her right from under his nose. It was only due to unfortunate circumstances they'd found each other again. "I love you with all my heart," Whit whispered in her ear.

Bonnie wriggled closer. "I love you too," she whispered back. "There's something I need to tell you, Whit," she said quietly.

His eyes stared into hers, and he knew it was something good. "Go on, then," he said, impatient to find out what he needed to know.

It was then he felt a slight movement. He wasn't sure what it was, though. Bonnie was beaming at him. "Is that what I think it is?" he asked, excitement filling him.

"It is," Bonnie said, joy in her voice. "We're going to have a baby."

Whit's heart was filled with happiness.

Epilogue

Two years later…

Bonnie stood in the doorway of the bedroom she once shared with Angus. Since his birth, it had been their son's room. It would soon be shared with his new brother or sister. Whit stood behind her, his arms wrapped around his wife, resting them on her very swollen belly.

"We did good," Whit whispered in her ear, so as not to waken their boy. It was then he felt their newest addition kick. "Not long now," he said, anticipation in his voice. "Are you ready for this?"

"I don't think I'll ever be ready," Bonnie told him. "Especially if it's another mini Whitney Starkey." She raised her eyebrows at him. "Your son wants to be like his Papa—riding horses, mucking out the stables, working the ranch." She rolled her eyes then, and leaned back into him.

Whit grinned at her words. But it was short lived. "I feel suddenly tired," Bonnie told him. "I need to lay down."

He knew exactly what to do, since this was the same pattern as when their first child was born. Whit lifted Bonnie into his arms and carried her to bed. Ensuring she was comfortable, he ran outside and asked Buck to fetch the doctor. It wouldn't be long and their second child would be born.

Whit put plenty of water on to boil, anticipating the doctor's request, while Buck went to town and fetched Doc Tantor.

He gathered up as many towels as he could find, then went to sit by his wife's side. He was pleased to see she was sleeping. She needed to conserve her energy for the delivery. Childbirth was always risky, but Doc Tantor was the most highly regarded doctor in the county. Whit prayed he was available to deliver their latest child without issue.

He closed his eyes and silently prayed for a good outcome. He loved Bonnie more than life itself. He wanted the best for her, and prayed she survived the birth. When he opened his eyes, she was staring at him.

"What are you doing?" she asked quietly.

Whit studied her. What should he tell her? He knew the truth was always the best. "I was praying for your safety, and that of our baby," he said, his voice emotional, even to his own ears.

Bonnie lifted her head and leaned forward to kiss him. "We will be fine," she said, "but prayers are always gratefully accepted." Almost the moment the words were out, she cringed, and Whit knew he was right. His wife was in labor. It wasn't long before he heard the front door open, and Doc Tantor came rushing in.

~*~

Whit paced so much awaiting the birth of their baby he'd made a new pathway out the front of the house as he carried young Nicolas—so named after the sheriff who saved his wife from Gus Jensen. It seemed like hours, and Buck tried to calm him down, but Whit knew the risks. Especially out here in the wilderness, away from town.

Finally, the front door opened. "It's a girl," the doctor announced cheerfully. "Mother and baby are fine. Whit, you can come in now, if you'd like."

If he'd like? Of course he wanted to go in. He needed to see for himself that his soulmate, the only woman he had ever loved, was in perfect health. Buck took Nicholas from him, and Whit went to his wife.

He paused at the doorway to their bedroom. Bonnie lay on the bed, their baby daughter in her arms. He couldn't help but take in the wonderous scene before him. He closed his eyes and gave thanks to the Lord above for keeping his family safe.

He finally stepped into the room and next to the bed, where he kneeled down and kissed Bonnie gently on the forehead. "Meet our daughter, Rose," Bonnie told him.

He stared into the baby's face. She was the image of her mother. He wouldn't have it any other way.

From the Author

Thank you so much for reading my book – I hope you enjoyed it.

I would greatly appreciate you leaving a review where you purchased, even if it is only a one-liner. It helps to have my books more visible!

About the Author

Multi-published, award-winning and bestselling author Cheryl Wright, former secretary, debt collector, account manager, writing coach, and shopping tour hostess, loves reading.

She writes both historical and contemporary western romance, as well as romantic suspense.

She lives in Melbourne, Australia, and is married with two adult children and has six grandchildren, and twin great-grandchildren.

When she's not writing, she can be found in her craft room making greeting cards.

Links

Website: *http://www.cheryl-wright.com/*

Facebook Reader Group:
https://www.facebook.com/groups/cherylwrightaut hor/

Join My Newsletter:

https://cheryl-wright.com/newsletter/
(and receive a free book)

www.ingramcontent.com/pod-product-compliance
Lightning Source LLC
Chambersburg PA
CBHW072148130726
47909CB00004BB/1258